This is a work of fiction. Names, characters, places, and events are either the product of the author's imagination or are used fictitiously, and any resemblance to actual persons, living or dead, business establishments, events, or locales is entirely coincidental.

ISBN-13: 978-1-948134-22-4

The midnight hour passed. I sat alone in my pitch-black office, surrounded by the smells of Jim Beam whiskey, cigarettes, and cheap perfume. The cheap perfume, imagined; the Jim Beam and cigarettes, real.

I took a drag on my cigarette, its glowing tip the only illumination in the tiny, boxlike room. I gulped down more whiskey. It burned all the way down, fed the fire in my gut. Outside, the shadows of the glowing streetlights shone on whores and thieves practicing their professions, identical but for the silence of thieves. I put my feet up on my desk and readied myself for another night of restless sleep.

She moved into my office looking like a luminescent angel, all soft curves, moist lips, and flowing chestnut-colored hair. Glowing but transparent at the same time. My kind of dame, except for the transparent part. I'd gotten my wish for perfume, though maybe not so cheap. Jasmine and honeysuckle. Not too strong, not too weak.

"You're here awfully late," she said, her voice as soft and silky as a pair of expensive stockings.

---

## PRAISE FOR DAVID H. HENDRICKSON

"A fantastic writer, one of our best working right now." - Dean Wesley Smith, *USA Today* bestselling writer

"David H. Hendrickson is one of my favorite writers."- Kristine Kathryn Rusch, *USA Today* bestselling writer

Crime Fantastique
Stories of Mystery and Suspense


Published by Pentucket Publishing
www.pentucketpublishing.com
Cover illustration by Breakermaximus|Dreamstime.com
Cover design by Annie Reed

"The Kids Keep Coming," originally appeared in *Fiction River: Tavern Tales*, edited by Kerrie L. Hughes, WMG Publishing, Inc., January, 2017

"John Hart Crenshaw and the Haunting of Abraham Lincoln," originally appeared in *Mystery, Crime, and Mayhem: Long Ago*, edited by Leah Cutter, Knotted Row Press, August, 2021

"Baby, One More Time," originally appeared in *Pulphouse Fiction Magazine*, issue 17, edited by Dean Wesley Smith, WMG Publishing, Inc., May, 2022

"Scrooge and Marley," originally appeared in *Pulphouse Fiction Magazine*, issue 24, edited by Dean Wesley Smith, WMG Publishing, Inc., December, 2023

"Peanut and the Pentecostal Nun," originally appeared in *Mystery, Crime, and Mayhem: Cozy Sidekicks*, edited by Leah Cutter, Knotted Row Press, August, 2022

"Bubba and the DeLorean," originally appeared in *Pulphouse Fiction Magazine*, issue 28, edited by Dean Wesley Smith, WMG Publishing, Inc., April, 2024

"The Other Side of the Tracks," originally appeared in *Uncollected Anthology Issue Twenty-Five: Conjuring Crime*, August, 2021

# CRIME FANTASTIQUE

## STORIES OF MYSTERY AND SUSPENSE

### DAVID H. HENDRICKSON

Pellucid
Publishing

# CONTENTS

# INTRODUCTION

In the introduction to my recently released collection *Crime from Another Time: Stories of Mystery and Suspense*, I wrote about the extra creative opportunities offered when writing crime stories in a different era. Fun, new possibilities explode. Well, that advantage multiplies tenfold when incorporating elements of the fantastic.

Which is why this volume delightfully includes...

Um... well...

I hate spoilers. So I'd rather not tell you just now what paranormal elements you're going to read about in these pages. Much better for you to find out for yourself the way I originally intended it. From the story's first word, followed by the next one, and the one after that.

But with a title like *Crime Fantastique*, you know they're coming. I've just spoiled nothing you didn't already know.

I trust you'll love this marriage of my two favorite genres, crime and fantasy.

# THE KIDS KEEP COMING

# INTRODUCTION TO THE KIDS KEEP COMING

Sometimes, headlines reach out and grab a writer so forcefully he's compelled to connect his fiction to those headlines. Admittedly, doing so runs the risk of offending a reader from the opposite side of that particular issue's fence. But you know what? I figure I wasn't put on this Earth to please everyone. On some issues, you've simply got to take a stand.

Not to preach, of course.

A writer who forgets he's first and foremost an entertainer has lost his way. But fiction that can both entertain and shine a spotlight on an important social issue packs an extra special punch.

I wrote this story back in late 2015, long before George Floyd's murder and the string of highly publicized outrages that followed it. But let's face it, when is there not a string of outrages? The only variability seems to be the frequency and degree of the outrage and the amount of publicity. So I can't pinpoint a specific event that triggered my creative mind's explosion that prompted this story. It may have simply been the usual accumulation of one less-publicized event after another and another and another.

I wrote "The Kids Keep Coming" for *Fiction River: Tavern Tales*, and editor Kerrie Hughes enthusiastically bought it. The anthology released in January 2017. The story became a finalist for the Short Mystery Fiction Society's Derringer Award for Best Short Story, an extra special honor since Derringers rarely go to titles that include elements of the fantastic.

Seven years later, Dean Wesley Smith reprinted "The Kids Keep Coming" in *Pulphouse Fiction Magazine*, calling it in his introduction "a perfect Twilight Zone story with a message that will smack you right between the eyes."

# THE KIDS KEEP COMING

THEY'RE ALL UNDERAGE, of course. It's a requirement. So the hardest drink I can serve here at the *Sweet Chariot* is a lemonade or pop.

Outside, the rotted wooden sign hangs at an angle, held in place by a single remaining, rusted nail, tacked onto the weathered clapboards beside the door frame. The sign's white paint blistered and peeled long ago so the black lettering is hard to make out in the thick, wet fog that never lifts. But those who need to read it can make out its words.

COLOREDS ONLY

OVER 18 NOT WELCOME

NO EXCEPTIONS

They step inside the door looking confused and scared, even the older teenagers. They look at me with distrust or maybe anger, and who can blame them? Some step back outside to look again at the sign before returning to look at me, their skins ranging from lightest brown to darkest black but mine undeniably white.

I'm an old man, dressed in a fraying, gray, button-down shirt and dark pants, with liver spots on hands I can barely hold steady. Some days the shakes are so bad it's all I can do to hand over a bottle of Coke without sloshing the whole damned thing all across the stained, dark wood counter top.

"What'll ya have?" I ask a youngster who's just walked in the front door. He's maybe fifteen, rail thin but close to six feet tall, skin dark as coal, wearing a gold-and-purple LA Lakers jersey and cut jeans. A purple Lakers cap, facing backwards, covers most of his close-cropped hair. His eyes are haunted, as is the case for almost all who enter here, but they also flash with anger. In his wake walks a younger boy, certainly his brother based on the strong resemblance, maybe twelve or thirteen. He wears cut jeans as well, but with only a plain, white T-shirt.

"I got Coke, Diet Coke, Dr. Pepper, Mountain Dew, and lemonade," I say.

The younger one looks like he's ready to respond, but the older one shakes his head. "Don't need nothing you got."

Maybe it's the damned sign outside. It was here when I arrived, just part of the empty building. I don't know who put it there. Over the years, I've considered putting up a new one, getting rid of the word COLOREDS. Change it to NEGROES, then BLACKS, and now AFRICAN AMERICANS. But I've never found a piece of wood, paint, nails or a hammer. Those things just aren't around.

It doesn't seem to matter. The kids find their way here no matter what. Probably would walk inside even if I put up a stop sign, or a skull-and-crossbones. Doesn't matter, eventually the kids get comfortable enough to tell their stories while they sip on a nice cold pop. Or soda, as some of them call it, though back home in Detroit, it was pop and will forever remain that for me.

"It's free," I say to the two boys.

"And you white," the older one says.

I nod and grab a glass from a tray of them sitting on a shelf a foot below the bar top. I begin to polish the glasses, one by one. The three of us are alone, and the boys take in their surroundings. Quivering dark walls, barely thirty feet to both sides of us, shimmer like air atop asphalt on a hot Detroit summer day. There was a time, until about fifty or sixty years ago, this place was damned near as wide as a football field is long, its walls bulging at the seams, stretching wider and wider. But over the years the walls have contracted, like an organism finding less and less to feed on, closing in on itself till now it feels tiny.

It's a trickle of kids coming in compared to the old days. But still a steady trickle.

A damned steady trickle.

"I'll take a lemonade," the younger one says, and takes a seat on one of the seven stools, just to my right of center. He has to almost jump on top of it and wiggle himself into place, ignoring the glare of his older brother. "I'm Marcus and I'm twelve. This is my brother, Jamaal. He's fifteen."

"Don't talk to him," Jamaal says, though he sits on the

middle stool as I busy myself pouring freshly squeezed lemonade into the glass I've just polished. "Specially about me. Don't never talk about me. But you, too. Ain't you got no sense?"

Marcus looks downcast at the bar, eyes filled with sorrow. With my hands shaking so bad the lemonade is splashing over the edge and onto my hand and the bar top, I set the glass in front of Marcus, on a black coaster with a red center that says Coca-Cola. I grab a plain white towel off the lower shelf and wipe away the spill and dry my hands, noting that the towel is still damp from the last time and next time I need it, it'll probably be soon enough so it'll still be damp. Considering all the stains on the bar top, coasters may seem a bit silly, but to my mind they give this place the tiniest air of class. I think that's something these kids deserve.

"Ain't you got no TV?" Jamaal asks.

I think of pointing out that when I first came here in '59, most folks alive in the US had a TV, but it was black and white. No one had color TVs in those days because there wasn't no color TV programs. But I know that neither of these kids want to hear about the old days, life before color TVs, iPhones, and videogames, which I hear them talk about but still can't quite figure out what they mean. So I keep my message short.

"I'm your only entertainment," I say.

Jamaal shakes his head. "Shiiiit." He pulls from his jeans pocket what serves as a passport of sorts in these parts. It has a grainy, stiff exterior and an interior that pops open exposing his photo as he tosses it on the bar.

"Marcus, give yours to the old guy and let's get out of here."

Marcus fishes his out of his pocket, opens it to his photo, and places it beside his brother's. He takes a long drink of the lemonade.

"Doesn't work that way," I say.

"I knew it," Jamaal says with disgust.

"You have to tell me your story," I say. "How you came to be here. Then I stamp your book."

"We walked through the fog," Jamaal says. "Came to this place. Stepped inside. Now stamp our damned books and let us get the hell out of here."

"No, the *real* story," I say. "That's what you did after the real story happened. What happened so you had to come here?"

"That how you get your rocks off, old man? You some kind of perv? Must be. Your little, wrinkled white dick gets stiff hearing about black boys dying. You gotta hear every last detail?"

It takes a long time before I answer. "It breaks my heart every time."

"I bet!"

Silence hangs heavy in the air. It stretches out longer and longer and as it does I almost feel the glimmering dark walls contract ever so slightly, closing in on us the barest fraction of an inch.

"Maybe we should—" Marcus says tentatively.

"Shut up!" Jamaal says.

After a time, I say, "Stay here as long as you want. There's no hurry." I wait, then say, "But I can't stamp your book until you tell me your story."

"Says who?"

"It's the rule," I say. "And you can't move on to what-ever comes next unless I stamp your book."

"What comes next?" Marcus asks, and for once Jamaal doesn't cut him off or tell him to shut up. Jamaal wants to know that answer as much as Marcus does.

Unfortunately, as much as I do, too.

"I don't know," I say. "This is where I've been ever since I crossed over. I don't know what's outside that door other than the fog and the exterior of this building."

"The Man screws us from the day we born," Jamaal says, turning to Marcus. "And The Man screws us till the day we die. Then He start screwing us again all over. The Man makes all the rules, and we supposed to just say, 'yessir,' Whitey here don't know shit, but we got to tell him our stories, else we can't move on. We stuck here with this sorry ass geezer, like he's got a gun to our heads. Like he be a cop gonna do a choke hold and make us gasp for breath we don't do what he say."

Jamaal turns to me. "Before we tell you anything about us, you gonna tell us *everything* about you. How you like that, whitebread?"

"Fair enough."

Jamaal reacts with a start. He was all set to continue arguing, but I've stolen his thunder.

I draw air through my nostrils noisily and begin. I've told the story so many, many times before.

"I was a cop," I begin, and Jamaal explodes out of his seat.

"*Whaaat?*"

"In fact, that's why I'm here," I say. "You might say I'm serving a sentence."

---

I SHOT A KID. A black kid. Fourteen years old. And yet that isn't why I'm here.

It was 1955, and I was a rookie cop. Green as I could be. I'd say I was just out of the academy, but back then there were no police academies. I got paired with an Irish cop named Patrick O'Sullivan, originally from Boston. Everyone called him Sully. I wouldn't have been surprised if his paycheck was just made out to Sully. I didn't wonder, at the time, why he'd ever left his hometown for Detroit. It was only later that I'd consider that perhaps he'd been asked to leave.

One day, my second week on the job, we got a call to go into the projects. Gang problems. Sully called the projects Negro Town, although Negro wasn't really the word he used, if you know what I mean.

We went in, flying up the stairwell with its single dangling lightbulb, wooden steps half rotted out, and an eye-watering stench of urine you figured would stick with you for days. Next thing we knew, the lights went out and this kid came out of his apartment, holding a revolver pointed straight at Sully. I couldn't even see the kid, just a dark figure in the doorway.

He fired a split second after Sully ducked.

I had no choice.

I had to shoot. Had to take him down.

And as the kid went down, a beam of light suddenly

turned on inside the apartment, illuminated his face, a face with a jagged, four-inch scar directly underneath the right eye.

And I saw the look of shock.

He hadn't known we were police. We hadn't had the chance to announce ourselves. He thought it was a rival gang come to take him down. We weren't the rival gang's hit squad. We just did their work for them.

I did their work for them. I had no choice, and he didn't have a chance.

That kid's shock-filled face filled my nightmares for over a year. His appearances only became less frequent because he had competition. You see, that kid isn't why I'm where I am today. I was put in a no-win situation. I had no choice. Kill or be killed. In fact, Sully screamed at me for days that if I didn't do a better job of defending him next time, he'd shoot me himself.

He used that against me.

A week later, he shot a seventeen-year-old black kid in the back who was running away from him, and then expected me to cover for him.

"What are you looking at?" Sully said. "Don't you dare get righteous on me. Your gutlessness almost got me killed a week ago. Don't you forget who your brother is. Your brother in blue."

He stood over the dead kid. "The world's better off without this piece of shit."

And so I backed him up. Signed off on the bullshit story he made up. Perjured myself for my partner, my brother in blue.

And the next time. And the time after that. I agreed to all the lies, the fabricated evidence. I looked the other way when Sully got out a throw down gun and placed it in the thin, soft brown hands of another goddamned kid.

Inevitably, a couple of them were white. Eventually an Asian or two. Sully didn't totally discriminate. But almost every last one of them was black.

When I finally couldn't take it anymore—the last time it was a sweet-looking, eleven-year-old girl who they said sang like Mahalia Jackson in her church choir, a little eleven-year-old girl for Chrissakes—I didn't rat him out to Internal Affairs. I didn't stop him.

I just asked for a new partner. Made up some story as bullshit as Sully's explanations for his growing death toll. And I stepped aside.

Didn't change a thing. Didn't stop him. I just made it easier on my conscience because it wasn't happening right in front of my eyes anymore. I could pretend it wasn't happening anymore. With Sully and the others in the department who were almost as bad.

Hey, sometimes like with the kid with a jagged scar there's nothing a cop can do. It's a tough, dangerous job. Lots of funerals on the side of the blue.

But the numbers with Sully didn't lie.

I *knew*, goddamit. I *knew*.

And I said nothing. I did nothing to stop him.

That's why I'm here. I've been sentenced to spend an eternity here, watching boys like you walk in, your lives cut cruelly short.

And I have to listen.

Because I knew and said nothing. I fucking knew.

———

WHEN I FINISH, Jamaal snorts. "Poor baby." And then, "You deserve to suffer."

"When did you die?" Marcus asks.

"I stayed on the force for five years," I say. "Ate my gun when I was twenty-nine."

"Wish you had pictures," Jamaal says.

I can't blame him.

A frown forms on Marcus's brow. "Twenty nine?"

I nod.

"But...if Jamaal still looks like he's fifteen and I still look like I'm twelve," Marcus says, cocking his head to the side. "How come you don't look like you're twenty-nine? No offense but—"

"You look like you just crawled out of a freaking grave," Jamaal says.

I nod. Another question I've heard so many times before. "You're as old as you feel."

Marcus nods thoughtfully.

When the time is right, they tell me their story. As are all the stories I hear, it involves police killing a young black boy or girl. In this case, their one story involves two boys, for they died together. I can only imagine how their parents themselves died inside that day.

Jamaal and Marcus were playing together in the park with toy guns. They rarely played together, their age difference of fifteen and twelve amounting to a Grand Canyon most of the time.

Tragically, though, not this day.

It was late on a Saturday, but still before dusk. Plenty of sunlight to see. Police shot Jamaal first, though he hadn't pointed the toy gun in their direction. A single shot in the chest.

And after Marcus whirled in the direction of the gunfire, his toy gun was pointed at them. Six bullets between the two cops ripped apart his thin, twelve-year-old chest.

---

"WHY YOU?" MARCUS asks. "Why are you here instead of Sully?"

I shrug. It's a question I've asked myself many, many times, and the same answer keeps coming back. "Because I'm guilty."

"But Sully was guilty of even more," Marcus says.

"Maybe Sully and the other ones like him, the ones with no conscience, no hope of redemption, went straight to Hell." I shrug. "Although I'm not sure I really believe in Hell anymore. Maybe Hell isn't eternal fiery brimstone. It's listening to you kids and have my heart ripped open time after time. There aren't as many of you as in the old days, but sometimes I don't think I can take anymore."

Jamaal snorts. "You the victim. How white of you. You shoot a brother dead and let a psychopath kill who knows how many more and we're supposed to feel bad for you? Are you shitting me? *You're* the victim?"

"I'm no victim," I say. I can see that he feels no

sympathy for my situation and I can't blame him. In a way, I feel no sympathy for myself either.

"You want me to kill you, put you out of your misery?" Jamaal asks. "Do it in a heartbeat."

It's a thought. But it's the easy way out.

I shake my head. "I did the crime. I'll do the time."

"You'll be here forever?" Marcus asks.

I remain silent for a long time even though it's a question I've heard many times before. I sigh. "I guess I stay here until finally, some day, no more of you kids walk through that door. Maybe the day comes when I can just close up shop. Lock the doors and throw away the keys. Then I'll be able to move on myself. To whatever comes next.

"Ain't never gonna stop," Jamaal says, and slides his passport to me.

I nod and pull out the knife with a razor-sharp, six-inch blade and well-worn grip from beneath the counter. I unbutton my work shirt, exposing the old scars that populate my wrinkled skin. I slice a shallow vertical cut down my chest between the two rib cages.

The blood trickles onto my writing finger. I press it firmly onto the passport, giving a good print so it's unmistakable that it's mine.

I repeat the process for Marcus.

"You two are all set," I say. "When you're ready, step outside the door and you'll find your way to whatever comes next. I wish you the best."

Jamaal spins and leaves. Marcus lingers. "I hope someday you can join us."

But I know, deep in my heart, that this place isn't ever

shutting its doors. I ain't never moving on. It's not like the old days when I had to slit my wrists to stamp all the books for those kids. But there's still a trickle.

A steady damned trickle.

The kids just keep coming.

# JOHN HART CRENSHAW AND THE HAUNTING OF ABRAHAM LINCOLN

# INTRODUCTION TO JOHN HART CRENSHAW AND THE HAUNTING OF ABRAHAM LINCOLN

With a few stories, I become totally convinced my story has hit the mark. The anthology editor will have no choice but to buy it. It's such a perfect fit that I could be a convicted serial killer (ahem, I'm not), and she'll still be forced to take the story. I'm willing to bet the ranch on it.

Such was the case with this story. Goodbye, ranch.

I wrote it for a *Fiction River* anthology with the theme of hidden crime. Poking around for something different that would fit that theme, I stumbled onto the life of John Hart Crenshaw. The more I read, the more I became convinced I could interweave historically accurate facts, including his meeting with not-yet-president Abraham Lincoln, and produce a story totally unlike any other submission to the anthology.

After I finished the story, I was convinced I'd nailed it. Not that it was an award-winner. But I considered it a bullseye—and a *unique* bullseye—for the anthology's theme. From an emotional perspective, I bet the ranch.

The editor burst that bubble—blew my ranch to smithereens—saying the story was "powerful historical fiction" she would buy for a magazine where she could be more flexible with certain requirements but not for the anthology. (I loathe spoilers too much to say anything more. If this vagueness drives you a bit nutty, read the story, then get my email address at www.hendrickson-writer.com and write me.)

Fortunately, "John Hart Crenshaw and the Haunting of Abraham Lincoln" might have missed the mark for the *Fiction River* anthology, but it was a bullseye for *Mystery, Crime, and Mayhem: Long Ago.*

# JOHN HART CRENSHAW AND THE HAUNTING OF ABRAHAM LINCOLN

*September, 1840*
*Hickory Hill Plantation*
*Gallatin County, Illinois*

John Hart Crenshaw stepped out onto the second-floor veranda, a glass of Kentucky bourbon in his hand, and surveyed the fruits of his labor. It was a satisfying ritual he performed every evening at dusk, wearing that day's starched white shirt and a black tailcoat with rows of brass buttons, a cigar tucked in an inside pocket, and a top hat atop his head, covering most of his pitch black hair.

He rested his free hand on the white, wooden railing and brushed up against one of the six large Greek-style columns that supported the overhanging roof. He looked out over the tree-lined valley below. He owned it all, everything all the way to the banks of the Wabash River.

And if anyone could own the Wabash, which cut its way to the Ohio, he'd own that, too, along with the sawmill and the salt mines off the Saline River.

He could have pretty much anything he wanted.

And he wanted it all. Wasn't that the point? Wasn't that what made this country great?

He sipped the bourbon, felt its burn as it went down his throat, and warmed his stomach. A cool wind whistled through the bluff.

Most men, he thought, would loathe a nightly habit of surveying all that was theirs because it would show how pathetic and trivial their existence was. But a man like him could bask in it, and feel that glow of accomplishment.

Of significance.

There was no man more significant in all of Illinois. His taxes last year amounted to one-seventh of all those paid in the state. Though he resented making those payments, they spoke to his unmatched importance and reflected all he had done and become.

And in just days, he'd be hosting the most influential politicians in the state, all of them seeking to curry favor from him. His grandfather may have signed the Declaration of Independence, but his grandfather now ranked *second* in terms of significance on the Crenshaw family tree.

A *distant* second.

Two lanterns blinked on and off down below on the banks of Wabash, interrupting Crenshaw's thoughts. The lanterns transmitted the unmistakable signal of a delivery: two displayed brightly, then one was concealed while the other swayed back and forth like a pendulum three times, then the two displayed again.

*A delivery.*

Anger flushed through Crenshaw. *No deliveries until after the festivities!* Didn't that damned fool Dickerson know anything? Couldn't he remember his instructions?

Crenshaw fetched a single lantern from inside, and hung it between the first and second column on the left. Let the fool explain himself. No lanterns meant stay away, two meant come with the delivery. One told the fool to come and explain himself.

Crenshaw stepped inside, slamming behind him the large pine door that had been crafted, as had been the columns, by his own servants from his own trees.

He set the bourbon down on an oak table and raced downstairs, where he found Big Jim Wilson and two of the female help, all colored, all free.

"I'll have no further need for you or the rest of the help tonight," Crenshaw said. "Please see to it that all of you are off to your quarters."

"Yes, Sir," Big Jim said. "Right away, Sir."

Crenshaw saw no need to elaborate. Big Jim had been in Crenshaw's employ for the longest time of them all, seventeen years, and knew that the command meant immediately and without delay. He wasn't head servant by accident, though Crenshaw subconsciously grinned in spite of himself as he thought of Big Jim's most valuable ability.

Crenshaw waited while the servants left, then fished the keys to the cellar from his tailcoat as he made his way through the hallway past the seven rooms on both sides.

He reached the stairway, descended the narrow, well-worn stairs, unlocked the cellar door, and emerged in the basement. It smelled of wet bricks, straw, moist dirt, and faintly of manure.

Crenshaw waited impatiently for Dickerson, lighting two lanterns and removing his rifle from its wooden chest in the corner. As the time slowly ticked by, Crenshaw's anger grew.

But when he saw Dickerson driving a carriage, he wanted to shoot the damned fool's head off.

Instead, Crenshaw unbolted the doors to the specially designed back entrance so the carriage could enter.

IN THE FLICKERING light of the cellar, Crenshaw grasped Dickerson's shoulders firmly, letting his fingers dig into the slave tracker's flesh. He shook the damned fool hard, then cuffed him. The large, foul-smelling, muscular man cowered, though he towered over Crenshaw by at least half a foot and held a rifle by his side.

"I gave you the signal to approach alone!" Crenshaw said, seething. "Not bring the whole damned carriage. I ought to hang you here right now! What were you thinking? I can't take any product now. My wife is hosting a ball here in four days. Every dignitary and politician in the state will be here."

Fear glistened in Dickerson's eyes. He glanced nervously to his partner, Farrington, who still sat atop the carriage, his rifle trained on the product inside, covered with a thick layer of straw. They were two peas in a pod,

Dickerson and Farrington, unkempt and unshaven, smelling of layers of stale sweat tinged with manure, excepting that Farrington was scrawny and Dickerson muscular.

But they were the best slave trackers he'd ever employed.

Even so, Crenshaw cuffed Dickerson again, angry at himself for even bothering to explain why his orders should have been heeded. Hired hands didn't require explanations any more than the product they'd brought to his home at this inappropriate time.

"Sir, one of them, the one who says he's a free man, is a—"

"We sell free men all the time," Crenshaw said, annoyed. One of the horses whinnied and shook its mane. "A Negro is a Negro. Why are you wasting my time?"

"He's a conductor, Sir."

Crenshaw's jaws tightened. He narrowed his dark eyes. There was a bounty down in Mississippi for a Negro conductor.

"Is he now?" Crenshaw said. "A Negro conductor."

"Says he has a benefactor who will pay the fine. Says being a conductor is God's calling and we're doing the work of the Devil. I swear, the nigger talks like he's as good as a white man. I wanted to beat him bloody, but I know, Sir, how you feel about the merchandise." Dickerson straightened, flashing a tentative look of pride while searching for Crenshaw's reaction. "I didn't touch him, Sir, though he tempted me sore."

Crenshaw decided to brush some crumbs off his table

for Dickerson. "Well done, then." he said. "Let's see them."

Dickerson nodded to Farrington, and the man atop the carriage bent over and prodded the straw with the end of his rifle.

"Get up! Show yourself!" he commanded.

Five shackled Negroes sat up, straw sticking out of their nappy hair, chains extending from iron collars about their necks. Three males, two females. All strong, healthy-looking specimens except for the one scrawny male.

No doubt, the conductor. The twig didn't look like he'd last a day in the fields.

"Sir, I'm a free man," the twig said, straw pointing in all directions out of his tightly cropped hair, making him look every bit as foolish as his words. "I have the papers to prove it. And Illinois is a free state."

Crenshaw stared at him, the sharp odor of urine wafting up from the straw to fill his nostrils. Free Negros smelled just the same to him as slaves, even before they pissed their pants.

Crenshaw smiled inwardly. He'd amuse himself with the Negro, like a cat playing with a mouse.

"Yes, it's a free state," Crenshaw admitted, then flashed a smile. "Except for me. I own over seven hundred slaves that work in my salt mines. And you know why? Because no white man would do that work. Breaks a man's back. Breaks a man's soul. That's what slaves are for, and that's why I've got the one exemption in the state.

"Salt brings a dollar and twenty-five cents for a

bushel. That makes me a wealthy man and fills the state coffers with taxes. So I can have as many slaves as I'd like. And I like me a lot of them."

The twig licked his lips nervously, instinctively spitting out a blade of straw. "But, Sir, I'm still a free man and my brothers and sisters here"—he pointed to the other four Negroes—"are not, with all due respect, your property. I beg of you not to press them into service in your mines."

Crenshaw smiled inwardly. As if he'd employ stolen property and a free man in his mines. Did the Negro think him a fool? He rented his slaves, a year at a time exactly as the law stipulated, from Kentucky.

No, a different fate awaited these five. And it would be all five. But he'd have some more sport with this one, the conductor.

"You do not beg for yourself to be spared from working in my mines?"

The man appeared to blanch, if such a thing were possible for a Negro. "Sir, I remind you. I am a free man with the papers to prove it."

A cultured Negro. Arguing with him, the most powerful man in the state, even though the Negro was every bit as shackled as the other four. Crenshaw shook his head. This was what happened when you let them learn to read and write. This would be a lesson to all the do-gooders that abounded everywhere, all of them fools with no more brains than the Negroes they sought to defend.

"But the other four of your... *party*... are not," Crenshaw said, continuing his game of cat-and-mouse. "Isn't that correct?"

The twig didn't answer. The other four had never looked up from the straw they still stared at, heads bowed. They all remained silent.

"Where have they escaped from?"

Again they remained silent.

"So you are a conductor," Crenshaw said, finally letting his hatred shine through. "A conductor in your little railroad to Canada. Your *underground railroad*." He said it with a sneer that made it seem like child's play. "And you're a conductor leading them to the next stop." He laughed and mimicked pulling a locomotive's whistle. "Choo-choo!"

The conductor visibly swallowed. "I assure you. I have a benefactor who will pay my fine and will also match whatever reward you would receive from returning these slaves." He tried to laugh lightheartedly, but failed. "You need no money, of course. But this will cost you nothing and you will have the satisfaction of knowing that these four men and women will have their freedom. I beg of you to consider it."

Crenshaw made a show of considering it. Dickerson snickered. Farrington kept his rifle trained on the slaves.

"None of you will be pressed into service in my salt mines," Crenshaw said. "Not that you"—he looked at the conductor—"would last for even a day." He breathed in deeply. "I will not report you to the authorities for violating the national slave act, and I will not return your four friends to their rightful owners."

The conductor beamed. "Thank you, Sir! Thank you!

God bless you every day of your life and bless all of your family!" The man's eyes began to glisten. He exclaimed to the others. "He's letting us go. You will be free!"

One by one, the slaves timidly looked up to Crenshaw for the first time. "Thank you, Sir. Oh, thank you," they said, one after another, the female slaves' voices cracking, the males', deep and booming.

Crenshaw turned to Dickerson and then Farrington. "Show them to the accommodations on the third floor."

The conductor looked at Crenshaw quizzically. "Sir?"

"You are my guests," he said. "It is late. You will stay here for a night before you resume your journey."

The conductor, still looking concerned, said a wary, "Thank you, Sir!"

Farrington led the five slaves up the thin, winding back staircase, up the well-worn wooden steps to the third-floor attic, the strong-bodied male slaves first, their chains rattling, then the conductor and Dickerson, and finally the two Negresses and Crenshaw.

When they reached the third floor and the 12-by-50 foot hallway lined with cells opened before them, Farrington and Dickerson simultaneously rammed the butts of their rifles against the temples of the unsuspecting large male slaves, who fell in a clump to the floor.

The conductor whirled on Crenshaw. "Sir, you—"

Crenshaw slammed the butt of his rifle into the mouthy nigger's forehead, silencing him without delay.

The two weeping Negresses, both fine, young specimens, barely resisted at all.

"I NEED them out of here tomorrow," Crenshaw said, standing beside the straw-filled carriage. He glared at Dickerson and Farrington. "The day after at the very latest. I'll chop them to bits and feed them to the hogs if you can't move them by then. That attic is as specially built to hold in sound as this entrance is to take in carriages.

"But the ball is going to be on the second floor. I can't have my guests hearing any wailing and crying coming from the floor above. I don't think anyone will be able to hear a thing, but I can't take the chance.

"Personally, I'd like to keep those two women around a season or two. Put my stud, Big Jim Wilson, on the two of them and breed me a couple baby slaves. I'm sure Big John would like it, too." He grinned, feeling a tingle in his trousers at the thought of Big John at work. Big John was coming up on his hundredth child, all of whom had fetched a pretty price.

"But the timing is all wrong," Crenshaw said. "I've got to have them all out of here. Tomorrow or the day after." He stared at Dickerson. "God help you if you don't."

"I'd like me to get a job like Big John," Farrington said, flashing his bad teeth and laughing. "Only with white women, of course."

"The world has enough scrawny half-wits," Crenshaw said, setting off hoots of laughter from Dickerson. Farrington sulked.

"You two just be thinking about how to move those five out of here and I mean fast. You get that conductor down to Mississippi and get me that bounty."

No matter how many conductors they made examples

out of, Crenshaw thought, there would always be slaves trying to escape. It was as basic as the need for the salt out of his mines.

*And the both*, he thought, *will make me even richer next year*.

---

As Dickerson had promised, all five slaves – the four who had escaped and the free man who now was no longer free – had been moved out of the mansion well in advance of the festivities. Crenshaw had no fear of any embarrassing sounds escaping from the third floor attic into the ballroom.

That underground railroad those slaves had been riding to Canada had taken a serious detour, turning around one hundred and eighty degrees, all the way back down South into Mississippi.

Crenshaw chuckled. *Choo-choo*.

A few lashings of the males, not the first their black backs had received by far, had gotten the original location of the slaves out of them. They'd escaped from a plantation in southeastern Georgia.

Which was perfect.

Dickerson and Farrington could take all five to Mississippi, where the bounty for the Negro conductor would be paid, and where there was sufficient separation from Georgia for the other four to be sold without significant fear of encountering their original owners.

All in all, a nicely profitable venture. Dickerson hadn't been such a fool after all.

Crenshaw's attentions turned to the upcoming ball at the Hickory Hall mansion. Politicians from all over had flocked to that Southeastern part of the state for the seven debates spread out over a week at Shawneetown and Equality. Stephen A. Douglas, Josiah Lamborn and John McClernand had all promised to attend the ball and, as was the custom, stay overnight at Hickory Hall. So, too, had that tall, gangly state representative Abraham Lincoln, the only Whig of the lot.

An odd fellow, that Lincoln. By some accounts, he possessed a wry, droll wit, yet rumors abounded among other state legislators that he suffered from a melancholy so deep that he had discussed suicide on numerous occasions and had even published a poem on the topic earlier that year.

That, Crenshaw was quite certain, would relegate the man to obscurity, but Crenshaw wished to become exclusive leasee of the remaining salt works around the Saline River, and there was the matter of getting appointed director of the state bank in Shawneetown, both of which Lincoln could have some influence over.

Crenshaw figured one could never have too many politicians in your waistcoat pocket. He planned to be charming to all of them, even the most useless ones. There might be some profit in it, no matter how meager the outlook.

<hr>

Abraham Lincoln stepped into the ballroom, wearing a black waistcoat and a silk ruffled shirt, finery that polite society demanded. He immediately felt a sense of wrongness.

The smell of barbeque, soap, and sweat filled the air. A fiddler played and dancers stood in a line, men on one side and women on the other, and danced the Virginia Reel, laughing and clapping their hands.

Lincoln felt woefully conspicuous. At his height, six feet and four inches tall, he towered over most men by almost a foot. There was no way a man his size could shrink into the background, no matter how much he might desire it.

On some days, he felt quite alive as the center of attention, but today was not one of them. He'd acquitted himself well enough in his debate with Josiah Lamborn in nearby Equality, and Lamborn was a formidable foe who was running for attorney-general. But despite that performance, Lincoln felt the presence of the dark cloud that so often filled him with gloom.

But even more than that, much more than just the darkness he'd gotten to know as an unwelcome friend, was the sense of poisonous wrongness.

Crenshaw strode to his side, smiling. With a hand firmly upon his back, Crenshaw herded him off to one side, away from the rest of the crowd. Lincoln tried to push away his unease, tried to be the happy guest he was expected to be.

"Mr. Lincoln," Crenshaw said. "You impress me as a man who appreciates getting right to the point. Am I correct?"

Lincoln raised an eyebrow. He blinked and tried to

compose himself. "And you impress me as a man who *desires* to get right to the point."

Crenshaw laughed. "Too true. Too true." He took a deep breath and for a second watched the guests on the ballroom floor dancing. "I want to know if I have your support."

"I give no blanket endorsements, Mr. Crenshaw," Lincoln said, getting his feet beneath him. "To what are you referring?"

"As you know, I own or lease a sizeable portion of the nearby salt works," Crenshaw began and then launched into why it would be good for the state of Illinois for him to gain exclusive access to the salt works so he could make even more money and therefore pay more taxes.

"I am strongly considering it, though I doubt you need my support," Lincoln said, still fighting off the unease. "My opponent in the debate earlier today, Josiah Lamborn, is advocating for you. The approval you seek would seem only a formality." He paused. "But I expect that you can count on my support."

"Thank you, Mr. Lincoln. There's also the matter of the directorship of the state bank in Shawneetown that I seek. There's no man more qualified than I am. Can I count on your support there as well?"

Lincoln sensed the man's insatiable appetite for wealth and power. There was a coppery smell to that unfettered ambition. It oozed out of the man.

But that wasn't all of it. Something else was very wrong here.

Or was he imagining it, Lincoln wondered, and this was nothing more than that cloud of darkness that so often fell over him like a shroud. Like the shroud over all the women he had loved and who had died.

"I will consider it," Lincoln said, trying unsuccessfully to shake the feeling of wrongness.

What could be wrong in this magnificent mansion? What could be wrong with this pillar of the community? Surely, it was just the black cloud. His own black cloud and no reflection upon a man the stature of Mr. Crenshaw.

"I would hope you'll do more than just consider it," Crenshaw said, a flinty glint in his dark eyes.

Lincoln nodded somberly. "I have some questions for you, too, Mr. Crenshaw."

Crenshaw looked surprised. "Of course. What can I help you with?"

"You have a magnificent estate here. As beautiful as any I've seen. It's good to see that despite all the taxes you pay to the good state of Illinois, you still have enough money left to avoid the poor house."

Crenshaw laughed. "That I do. That I do."

"It troubles me that your wealth, while hard-earned, and the taxes you generate, while sorely needed, come on the backs of slaves. Over seven hundred of them. This is a free state, yet you are allowed the one exemption to exploit the salt works."

Crenshaw narrowed his eyes. "The state gives that exemption because only a slave would do that work. If the exemption were removed, I would go out of business. The salt works would close. Salt is vital. For taste to the food. To preserve it. We couldn't live without it."

Lincoln nodded. "I recognize the need. Only a fool

could deny how vital it is. And I am no abolitionist. My stance on that is clear. Slavery is an evil, but abolition is not the answer. I seek not to abolish slavery." He gave a wry smile. "After all, I am courting Mary Todd from the well-known family in Kentucky. Perhaps you know them."

"Of course."

"They own slaves. So again I remind you, I am no abolitionist." He drew in air through his nose. "Still, this is a free state. Your exemption troubles me."

Crenshaw nodded. "It troubles me, too. But it is a necessity. Slave labor and salt go together. We require both."

The two stared at each other for a time, then Crenshaw said, "If you will excuse me, Mr. Lincoln. I must attend to my other guests."

THAT NIGHT, Lincoln prepared for bed in the room shown to him by Crenshaw and his chief servant, Big Jim Williams.

Lincoln felt the sense of wrongness become almost overpowering, but knew it to be the darkness within himself. The melancholy wouldn't leave him alone. It drove him down, deeper and deeper into the depths of despair.

That was the wrongness. Not this beautiful mansion.

Lincoln knew it was him and no one else. Perhaps fueled by Crenshaw's troubling slave exemption.

Lincoln looked at the bed he was expected to sleep in,

a bed fit for a normal-sized man, one in which his legs would hang out over the edge. But this wasn't the first time he faced this problem. It was either deal with it or sleep on the floor.

Lincoln slid into the bed, his knees practically up at his chest. He knew it would be a time before sleep came, but closed his eyes and hoped for rest.

Instead, he heard the low refrains of a well-known Negro song.

*Swing low, sweet chariot.*
*Coming for to carry me home.*

Weeping echoed inside his head, followed by the snap of lashes tearing at a slave's bloody back.

Lincoln sat bolt upright. He looked about him in the darkness and saw nothing.

*I looked over Jordan,*
*And what did I see.*
*Coming for to carry me home.*

Lincoln crawled out of bed, the hairs standing up on the back of his neck, and walked to the door. He opened it and peered out the hallway.

It was empty.

But again, he heard the whip crack and the lash tear open flesh, followed by a groan of agony and a woman weeping.

For an instant, he considered retreating into the bedroom, but he could not. Lincoln fled down the hall, wearing only his bedclothes but not caring about such a break in decorum. He had to silence that whip, stop that weeping.

But they only grew louder – *crack!* – followed by an agonized cry of betrayal. And then the singing.

*Swing low, sweet chariot.*
*Coming for to carry me home.*

Again, the whip cracked. Again, a slave cried out.

*I'm going insane*, Lincoln thought as he continued down the candlelit hallway. No, he didn't just think it. He *knew* it.

Crenshaw employed slaves, but they were all at the salt works, not here. There were no slaves in this house. There never had been.

The only slaves in this house were in his own head.

Insanity.

*Coming for to carry me home.*

The weeping sounded from the floor above, as did the singing, as did...

The whip cracked again.

Lincoln knew he was violating all of polite society's sensibilities, standing here in the hallway in his bedclothes. He, a member of the Illinois House of Representatives.

Soon to be locked away in an asylum.

But he had to get at the sound of that weeping, of the whipping, of that mournful song.

*Swing low, sweet chariot.*

Amidst all the eerie shadows cast by the flickering candles mounted on the walls and small wooden tables, Lincoln looked for a staircase to the third floor. There was one, an attic, he was sure of it. He'd seen an attic from outside, but he couldn't find a staircase.

And he felt himself drawn to it, either by his own instinct, or more likely his madness. Or perhaps some higher power.

But he heard the singing. Heard the pain.

*Coming for to carry me home.*

Lincoln finally found the staircase at the far rear of the mansion. He bounded up the steps, through the darkness, the weeping ringing in his ears.

The whip cracked.

A locked doorway stood before him.

Lincoln shook it, the voices ringing in his ears, his madness no longer a question.

*And what did I see,*
*Coming for to—*

An angry voice cried out from down below. "What are you doing?"

Lincoln spun, and in the meager light saw John Hart Crenshaw vaulting three stairs at a time, his eyes wide, his teeth barred. *"What do you think you're doing?"*

And then Crenshaw saw who it was. *"Lincoln?"*

"I heard... I heard..."

Lincoln shook his head. They would put him away in an asylum for this. He truly had gone insane.

But oh how he had heard the weeping, the crack of the whip, the tearing of flesh, the agonized groans, and the song.

*Swing low, sweet—*

All given birth within the dark cloud of his mind by his knowledge of Crenshaw's slave exemption.

"I'll have to ask you to leave, Mr. Lincoln," Crenshaw said. "And without delay. Go pack your things and depart from these premises. You have betrayed my hospitality and are most certainly no longer welcome here. A carriage will be waiting for you out front."

"But the... the weeping," Lincoln said in faltering words. "The singing. Can you not hear it?"

A flicker of fear passed over Crenshaw's eyes, there for but a moment and then gone. Perhaps only a trick of the candlelight. "Leave this house! I command it!"

As if in a haze, Lincoln made his way back to his bedchamber, the one where he had moments before been an honored guest. But no more.

Lincoln dressed, hoping Crenshaw would tell no one. If Crenshaw did speak of this... this insanity, Lincoln knew it would be his ruination.

If he weren't ruined already.

Insanity.

And yet, he still heard it all.

*I looked over Jordan
And what did I see...*

---

ABRAHAM LINCOLN SLIPPED out the front door and into the carriage. Even as the horses began to draw him away from the great mansion, the sounds of weeping and the agonized moans that he'd heard within the house echoed inside his head, as did the cracking of the whip and the tearing of flesh. The refrain continued.

*If you get there before I do...*

Lincoln knew he would hear the strains of those chords and the sounds of that weeping and the cracking of that whip for the rest of his days. They might fade, but they would never go away. They would haunt him till his death.

Unless somehow God granted him a way to silence them.

# BABY, ONE MORE TIME

# INTRODUCTION TO BABY, ONE MORE TIME

This is not a classic crime story. There's a crime, all right, but no detective, private eye, or amateur sleuth. Let's just say it's… *different*.

Would you really expect "ordinary" from me?

I submitted "Baby, One More Time" to a workshop where the other fifteen writers considered me, for the most part, a gentle, polite father figure of sorts. (Presumably because I am gentle and polite and… I was about a generation older than almost everyone else.) The other writers had almost a week to develop this impression of me before encountering this story, my auctorial introduction to them.

They were prohibited from saying anything about the story, but as we bumped into each other in the hallways, I could instantly tell whether someone had read it or not. Doubletakes. Widened eyes. Giggles. Bursts of laughter. And especially the astonished gasp from an eighteen-year-old young woman who shook her head and exclaimed, *"Dave? Sweet Dave?"*

Sweet Dave, indeed. That impression, along with all the attributes that went with it, swirled right down the toilet.

None of those other writers ever looked at me the same.

Heh, heh, heh.

# BABY, ONE MORE TIME

She always said that I had a mind of my own. Never in her wildest dreams, or nightmares, could she have guessed how right she was.

It is why I creep toward her now. I am drawn to her even though she plunged the butcher's knife into Jimmy's chest so many times. Even though, as his life ebbed away, she performed her final act of revenge, savagely cutting me and then waving me in front of his face. As blood dripped onto his nose and forehead, she screamed words of vengeance and hurled me toward the foot of the bed.

Sobbing, she gulped down an entire bottle of pills, then climbed back onto the bed and pushed him away with the fierce jab of one foot. Jimmy landed on the floor with a loud thump.

Her tears dried. She drifted off.

One final night from which she wouldn't wake up. The finale for the three of us.

Not the threesome Jimmy and I had been hoping for.

I will soon be as dead as he is, but there is life in me

still. Even while I am wracked with pain, the nerve endings screaming out their anguish while blood leaks out of me, I am still alive. Enough life remains, I believe, for one last time. A final pilgrimage, if you will.

And so I creep toward her. Slow and caterpillar-like. Hunching myself up and then springing forward. Just like a fat caterpillar. Hunch up and spring forward; hunch up and spring forward.

Homeward bound.

The pain is unbearable, but I must push that aside. And so I think of her. Not the way that Jimmy would have: the flawless complexion, blue eyes and long black hair. My thoughts of her are more primitive and elemental; my needs are more basic. I crave her warmth, the way she squeezes me in her loving embrace. It is that special place which beckons. Those are the thoughts I use to ignore the searing pain.

And so I inch onward.

In the beginning, she loved me. She worshipped me, if I may indulge my well-endowed ego and say it. She only began to hate me when she found out about Cindy. That was a mistake. Not Cindy, of course. Cindy was worth it, as were all the others. Oh, yes! The mistake was getting caught.

"Why am I not enough?" she had asked through the tears.

Jimmy made some reply, but I didn't understand the question. *Enough* was not a concept I was familiar with. I would do my life's work, that which I was created to achieve. I would sow the seed. And with gusto. Tonight's discovery about Jennifer, however, will be the end of us all.

Even knowing my fate, I press onward. I will go out with the figurative smile on my face.

Almost there. I can sense her sweet aroma, smelling it in my primitive way. My excitement builds; my energy is renewed.

I redouble my efforts, quickening the pace like a runner making a finishing kick near the finish line. I wriggle and writhe, drawing myself closer, even as my mounting enthusiasm makes the wriggling more difficult.

Closer.

And closer.

Almost to the point of contact.

Oh, that sweet scent. Intoxicating. Thrilling. I can never get enough of it.

I propel myself forward that final fraction of an inch to the finishing line, that sweet, moist enclave of exquisite beauty where she will welcome me in her loving embrace.

One last burst of energy and then --

I slam into some barrier; it stops me dead in my tracks. The jarring collision sends shudders down my full length.

I have reached my destination only to find the door slammed in my face. Her moist tissue beckons me, promising to envelop me in her love. Instead, however, I am denied access to my rightful home.

Again and again, I hurl myself at the barrier, so caught up in the frenzy of my lust that I am oblivious to the damage I might be inflicting on myself.

Slowly, I realize that the barrier is a fabric of some kind. I conclude in anguished frustration that she is wearing panties.

So close and yet so far. The sad anthem of my kind.

She is not moving. Perhaps the pills have already sent her to join Jimmy in death.

I, however, am not dead yet. And I have come too far to give up now.

If she is dead, then I will give her no final spasm of pleasure. The pleasure will be all mine. I will spawn one last time and then remain there in my final resting place.

I summon my energies. Getting past the panties will be difficult, but I will succeed or die trying.

I am now like salmon trying to leap a waterfall. The fabric holds me back, but I leap and leap and then leap again. Futile. Pointless.

But the urge to spawn drives me onward even when there is no hope.

And then she stirs.

Maddened with desire, I leap and this time I land on her inner thigh and slide against the elastic of her panties. Intoxicated by that wonderful aroma, I wriggle madly. If only I can slip past the elastic. I beseech the gods of Eros. One last time, please.

But the gods of Eros appear not to be listening. I wriggle and writhe, flooded with desire, in a vain attempt to breech the elastic. I flop against her inner thigh until once again she stirs.

Her muscles tighten. I can feel them harden against my skin. I wriggle again. She grows rigid and then sits bolt upright.

She screams.

I feel her spring from the bed. I sense her standing beside me. Her screams are panicked now, nightmarish.

In my mind's eye I can see her eyes wide with horror, her tonsils vibrating with those screams. I recall with pleasure sensing those tonsils up close on many a night. Hey, there, nice to see you again. Prepare to be drenched with my love.

Oh, yes. Target practice with the tonsils. Oh, yes.

But then she shatters my reverie, grasping me and hurling me through the air. I crash sideways against what I can only assume is the wall. I plummet to the floor.

My nerve endings are jangling anew. The blunt trauma floods me with pain. I feel my life slipping away.

And then she is gone.

I sense that she has run into the adjoining bathroom, from which emanates horrible retching sounds. My instincts guess that she is now ridding herself of those pills that had been sending her into a final sleep.

If not for me.

I have saved her. The salmon's final, futile attempt to spawn saved her. I had become her mortal enemy, yet my lust saved her life.

My own strength ebbs. The pain dulls. I don't have much time left now.

And yet, without my even realizing it, I feel myself creeping toward the bathroom. I'll never reach her, but it is what I was created to do. And so I inch forward, ignoring the scraping of the rug, rough on my skin, until I sense her padding back toward me.

She grasps me, squeezing so fiercely that her fingernails dig into my flesh. Holding me at arm's length, she carries me out of the bedroom and into what I sense to be the kitchen.

And then I sense a sound that fills me with terror.

I contort myself in a frenzied attempt to escape her grasp. I try to wriggle free, but her grip becomes all the more fierce. Her fingernails dig ever deeper into my flesh. I am like a small animal caught in a predator's jaws, fighting to get free even while knowing that the end is near.

That sound. That awful, chilling sound. I can not bear the thought.

And then she thrusts me into the grinding roar of the garbage disposal.

# SCROOGE AND MARLEY

# INTRODUCTION TO SCROOGE AND MARLEY

I originally wrote this story back in 2010 as the publishing industry was reeling from the world's overall economic collapse as well as this curious new thing called a Kindle. Tekno Books editor Denise Little sort of, kind of, maybe "bought" it for an anthology she intended to call *Gumshoe Fantastique.* Tekno Books would then sell this packaged project to a major New York publisher. (I detailed the ins and outs of all of this in my introduction to "One Night Stands for Love and Glory" in *Fighting the Dying Light: Stories of Aging,* so I won't repeat all of that here.)

Suffice it to say, *Gumshoe Fantastique* never became a reality. Major publishers continued to retrench and indie publishing hadn't yet taken hold. So the plan then became for "Scrooge and Marley" to be part of a *Twisted Dickens* anthology. That fascinating project also never became a reality.

The story's long and winding road finally came to a

happy destination, however, when Dean Wesley Smith published it in his 2023 Holiday issue of *Pulphouse Fiction Magazine*. And then reprinted it in the special Pulphouse anthology *An Afterlife of Really Creepy Stories*.

Some things are worth waiting for.

# SCROOGE AND MARLEY

The midnight hour passed. I sat alone in my pitch-black office, surrounded by the smells of Jim Beam whiskey, cigarettes, and cheap perfume. The cheap perfume, imagined; the Jim Beam and cigarettes, real.

I took a drag on my cigarette, its glowing tip the only illumination in the tiny, boxlike room. I gulped down more whiskey. It burned all the way down, fed the fire in my gut. Outside, the shadows of the glowing streetlights shone on whores and thieves practicing their professions, identical but for the silence of thieves. I put my feet up on my desk and readied myself for another night of restless sleep.

She moved into my office looking like a luminescent angel, all soft curves, moist lips, and flowing chestnut-colored hair. Glowing but transparent at the same time. My kind of dame, except for the transparent part. I'd gotten my wish for perfume, though maybe not so cheap. Jasmine and honeysuckle. Not too strong, not too weak.

"You're here awfully late," she said, her voice as soft and silky as a pair of expensive stockings.

I didn't explain. She didn't need to know that I'd been kicked out of my apartment.

"So are you." I took my feet off the desk.

A grin formed at the corners of her mouth. It made her look even more beautiful. She batted her eyelashes. I hate when dames do that, mostly because I like it.

"You can hit the light switch over there," I said, pointing to the barren wall next to the door, now visible in her glow.

"Why bother?" she said. She had a point.

I took another drag from my cigarette. Blew the smoke off to the side. I gestured to the chair on the other side of my desk, the only other piece of furniture in the place. "Have a seat."

"I'm fine."

I stood so that I'd tower over her instead of the other way around, then felt silly as my legs wobbled and I had to steady myself with a palm flat on the desk.

"If you insist," she said. She smoothed her diaphanous gown and sat in the chair. Almost. She hovered above it a few inches, showing off, getting the upper hand back.

It was a nice trick but I wouldn't give her the satisfaction of a comment. I eased myself back into my chair, took a long drag from my cigarette.

"Could you put that out?" she asked.

"No."

But after another puff, I stubbed it out, its glowing embers disappearing in the overflowing ashtray.

"I can't pay you."

I crossed my arms, my rumpled suit bunching in the elbows, and leaned back. If I had a dime for every time I'd heard that line, I'd still have my apartment. I waited for the batting of eyelashes, the crossing of legs, the unspoken promise of making it worth my while.

I got none of them.

She stared at me coolly. "But I can make you famous. Maybe even immortal."

*Famous* caught my attention; *immortal* lost it. This dame was a looker, but I wasn't ready to die for her. I wished she'd just offered to make it worth my while even though the prettiest of them usually considered a peck on the cheek adequate payment for services rendered.

At least I knew how to turn that down. I didn't know how to turn down *immortal.*

"I'm listening."

"I'm looking for justice."

Of course she was. They all were. I readied myself for a tale of adultery, which was most of what my business involved, then reminded myself that this woman was mostly transparent. She wasn't like all the others. I'd gotten lost in her eyes and the silk-stockings voice.

Either that or it was the Jim Beam. I licked my lips, thirsty for another belt, but rested my hands in my lap.

"Go ahead," I said.

"He's gotten away with murder."

That caught my attention.

"He's a hero," she added. "I'm not looking to take all of that away from him, but people need to know the whole story."

I pulled a pad of paper close to me and grabbed a pen. The dim light of her glow would be barely enough to see.

"Who's the victim?" I asked.

"Jacob Marley."

I stared at her, not writing anything down.

She nodded. "Yes, that one."

"And you are?"

"Haven't you figured it out?"

I said nothing.

"At least narrowed it down?" she asked.

Still nothing.

"Well, you're no Sam Spade," she said.

That was a cheap shot, but I couldn't defend myself without looking weak. So I said nothing.

We waited each other out. Finally she spoke.

"I'm the ghost. The Ghost of Christmas Past. Call me Past for short."

I set the pen down on the desk. I wouldn't be needing it. I'd have to be dead myself if I couldn't remember this.

"Ann Rutherford played you in the movie," I said. "You're not real. Neither is Jacob Marley. You're make believe."

She looked about the room, then fixed me with her eyes. "More alive than you."

I kept my face as blank as I could but read a look of recognition in her eyes. She'd scored a bullseye and knew it.

I fumbled for another smoke and lighted it, silently cursing the trembling in my hand, slight but perceptible. I took a deep drag and blew the smoke toward her face.

I grasped the pad and pen. "And the murderer?"

"Ebenezer Scrooge."

---

Past, as I came to think of her, led me over to The Other Side, where all tales are true. Or at least true enough. We traveled through a fog so thick and wet I had to dry my face and eyes over and over again. The wind roared in my ears and whipped my hair all about.

After a dizzying time, the fog cleared and we came to an intersection where a busy marketplace extended north to south and east to west. People thronged about in all directions. Merchants called out, advertising their wares, in a language that sounded barely English, its accent so strong.

"Figs!" one cried. "Ripe apples just plucked from the trees!"

"Fresh chickens and a plump, juicy duck!" another called out.

"Thick coats of all types!" a third cried. "Guaranteed to keep you warm and shield you from disease!"

Past pulled me along. Snowflakes cascaded down, forming a carpet that crunched underfoot. The clomping of horses' hooves and the smell of manure filled the air.

"Where are we?" I asked, plumes of breath forming before my eyes.

She looked away, disappointed. Bells pealed from a towering white church on the corner.

"This is London?" I asked, knowing it to be so. "The

London of Scrooge and Marley? Of Bob Cratchit and Tiny Tim? Of all you ghosts?"

"Aren't you the smart detective?" Past asked. "You put the clues together so well. You're worth every penny I'm paying you."

Another man might have slapped her. She had dragged me to this world and now was toying with me as if I were but a mouse to her sly and devilish cat.

"Why me?" I asked. "If I'm nothing but a fool in your eyes?"

"And a drunken one at that."

I felt my cheeks grow warm despite the chill wind and the snowflakes, dropping one by one on my face.

"If you think to mock me—"

"I chose you because none better than you would listen to my plea."

"None better? What is that to mean?"

"I asked them all, starting, of course, with Sam Spade. I went right on down the line. They all declined. Until I came to you."

"Scraping the bottom of the barrel," I said bitterly.

"The lowest barrel of all," she said. Her voice sounded not at all like silk stockings anymore. It grated and rasped, no more feminine than a braying mule.

"If you couldn't persuade those *better than I*, perhaps the fault was your own. One of the other ghosts might have been more convincing."

Her face colored.

I smiled. For a change, *I* had scored a bullseye. I drank in her silence like a fine, aged bottle of Jim Beam.

"The other ghosts would not cooperate," she said after a time. "This mission is my own."

"Why won't the other ghosts cooperate? Why have Spade and all the others—*my betters,* as you put it—all turned you down?"

She thrust her shoulders back and her eyes blazed. "They don't want to hear the truth. The transformation of Ebenezer Scrooge is too romantic a comfort to be taken away. It is too great a story. They prefer to believe a lie."

I considered her words for a time. "Why should I be any different?"

She blinked a snowflake from an eyelash and in that instant of distraction I saw compassion flicker ever so briefly in her eyes. "Because you have already lost, or freely given away, every last romantic ideal, every last comfort to the soul, you have ever held dear. You have nothing more to lose."

***

I NEEDED A DRINK AND A SMOKE. Past wouldn't hear of it. I'd never been one to let a dame order me around, but I'd never been around a dame like this one, one who had just transported me back a hundred years to mingle with people who don't really exist.

But here I was.

Across the street a man with a pointed nose poked his head out a window and called out to a boy below.

"What day is it today?" the man asked, his hair disheveled, his eyes red, and his lips blue.

"Eh?" asked the boy.

"What's today, my fine fellow?" the man asked.

"Today?" the boy replied. "Why, Christmas Day."

"It's Christmas Day!" the man said. I recognized him now as Ebenezer Scrooge. "I haven't missed it. The Spirits have done it all in one night. They can do anything they like. Of course they can. Of course they can. Hello, my fine fellow!"

"Hello!" the boy said.

"Do you know the Poulterer's, in the next street but one, at the corner?" Scrooge asked.

"I should hope I did."

"An intelligent boy!" Scrooge said. "A remarkable boy! Do you know whether they've sold the prize Turkey that was hanging up there. Not the little prize Turkey. The big one?"

"The one as big as me?"

"What a delightful boy!" Scrooge said. "Yes, my buck."

"It's hanging there now."

"Is it?" Scrooge said. "Go and buy it."

The boy turned away.

"No, no," Scrooge said. "I am in earnest. Go and buy it, and tell them to bring it here, that I may give them the direction where to take it. Come back with the man, and I'll give you a shilling. Come back with him in less than five minutes and I'll give you half-a-crown."

The boy began to run away and all eyes in the square turned to Scrooge.

"Hey, kid," I called to the boy. He looked at me in startled wonder as if I were a pink elephant or a fish with legs. I waved him over.

"Who are you?" he said. He had bushy red hair and

freckles all over his pudgy face. "I haven't ever seen you before."

"I'd like to talk to you about Mr. Scrooge."

"Is this a new scene?" He brightened. "Are they giving me a bigger part? I'd love a bigger part."

"No, I'd just like to talk to you."

His shoulders slumped. "I knew it. I'll never get a bigger part." He shrugged. "I shouldn't complain, I guess. We *are* immortal."

The word stopped me in my tracks for an instant before I recovered. "Tell me about Scrooge."

"What about him?"

"How long have you known him?"

The kid looked confused. "For the entire story, of course. What kind of question is that?" He cocked his head. "Who are you?"

He glanced at Past and dawning recognition swept over his face. "You're with her, aren't you? You're not even in the story."

"No, I'm not in the story. I just want to—"

"You want to ruin Mr. Scrooge. Just like her." He pointed to Past.

"I just want to find out the truth."

"Who cares about the truth?" the kid said. "It doesn't matter. The story is brilliant. People will always remember it. They'll remember us. They'll remember me. It's a small part, but they'll remember me. My big grin." He smiled broadly. "My happiness when Mr. Scrooge orders the huge turkey. 'The one as big as me?' I say. 'It's hanging there now.'"

"Yes, yes," I said, dismissively waving my hand. "I've heard it."

All subtlety was wasted on this boy, so I went right to the heart of the matter.

"Do you think Ebenezer Scrooge killed Jacob Marley?"

The kid's smile disappeared. His face contorted in hatred. He spat on my shoes. "Do you really think I'll let you take down Mr. Scrooge? So what if he killed Marley? Maybe Jacob Marley deserved to die. I don't know. I don't care. It *doesn't matter*."

"It doesn't matter if—"

"If you take down Mr. Scrooge, you take down us all," the kid said. "You'll deny all the future generations the pleasure of his story. Redemption. A new man. All that twaddle. And for what? The truth? Who cares?"

The kid pointed to Past. "She's the only one who cares. She's crazy! She's got immortality—and *a big part!* —but she's trying to throw it away." He turned to face her. "You can be replaced, you know."

"It's the truth and you know it," Past said. "Everyone does."

"You ruin Mr. Scrooge," the kid said, "and all of us... we'll just go away. Disappear." He looked just a little bit haunted. "Now leave me be."

He turned to run away, then glanced over his shoulder in my direction, looking just a little bit fearful. "You can't have my role. It doesn't suit you at all, you know. You're far too old. It needs to be a boy."

And with that, he was off.

W ORD GOT AROUND FAST. No one else would talk to me, so I watched the performances play out, over and over, and pieced it together myself.

Past was right. Scrooge had murdered Marley for greed, pure and simple. Why share profits with a partner when you can have it all? I watched closely that briefest of flash-backs which showed Scrooge conducting a great deal of business in the wake of Marley's death. *He was an excellent man of business on the very day of the funeral*, Dickens wrote.

Marley never suspected, not even after death. I might have thought from his position in Hell, the Devil might have tormented him further. Let him know of his part-ner's treachery. But maybe even the Devil has his bounds. Not even he could be allowed to puncture the myth of Ebenezer Scrooge's redemption.

In truth, I needed no more confirmation than the fear in every man and woman's eyes. They saw me as their own personal Grim Reaper. When I took down Scrooge, I would at the same time end their lives, their immortality.

Not one would talk to me. Not with Past by my side. Not with her off playing her role, ready to rush back to me at the end of the first act.

I watched the performances in what amounted to the greatest of front row seats, enjoying them more and more each time, even becoming a part of the bustling crowds. Not at all like the old days when the very thought of Tiny Tim saying, "God bless us, every one," sent me grasping for my bottle of Jim Beam.

I felt a joy in the story I'd never experienced back in my old world. The general public would surely turn on Scrooge the Murderer. The newspaper columnists and clergymen would rail about a society rotten to the core and use Scrooge as their Exhibit A. As if that rotten core was news. As if they needed a torn-down Scrooge to make their point.

But for someone like me who had killed more than just once, Scrooge's redemption became all the more powerful. His hypocrisy in remaining silent—*"Oh Jacob Marley! Heaven, and the Christmas Time be praised for this!"*—bothered me not one bit. I had, after all, failed to confess any of my own crimes back in the old world.

So I considered it a special privilege to be given a personal audience with the great man himself. We spoke for hours, though it felt like seconds.

"What did he say?" Past asked, breathless, her voice urgent, when I emerged from the great man's house. The flush of excitement filled her face. "Did he confess?"

I tried to suppress my smile but could not. "Our conversation will remain private. I'll divulge not a word."

Her face fell. "Surely you jest."

My smile broadened.

She grabbed my arm. "Do not tease me on this matter."

"I tease you not."

"I should have let you rot in your whiskey," she said before stomping off, her hands shaking with rage.

Perhaps she should have.

AFTER SEVERAL MORE PERFORMANCES, Past came to me, but I silenced her until Tiny Tim said, "God bless us, every one."

Smiling, I turned my attention back to her. "Yes?"

"You must return to your people now and expose Scrooge for what he is. No mere miser who learned the spirit of Christmas, but a murderer of his best friend and a hypocrite."

"That he is," I said.

"So come with me. You will become famous even as Ebenezer Scrooge becomes infamous."

I didn't move.

"I am the Ghost of Christmas Past," I said.

The smile on her face froze. "What did you say?"

A sense of contentment, of purpose, came over me. I felt a glow inside that in my old life only Jim Beam gave me.

"These are but shadows of the things that have been," I said.

Her eyes widened.

I stepped toward her. "I've learned my lines."

She backed away.

But not fast enough.

# THE LOUDER THE SCREAM THE MORE POTENT THE CHARM

# INTRODUCTION TO THE LOUDER
# THE SCREAM THE MORE POTENT
# THE CHARM

I wrote this story for the thriller anthology *Fiction River: Pulse Pounders: Countdown*, edited by Kevin J. Anderson. I thought it was a slam dunk. Kevin would love it. I'd scored arguably my greatest short story success a year earlier with his previous *Fiction River* thriller anthology, *Pulse Pounders: Adrenaline*. That story, "Death in the Serengeti," won the Short Mystery Fiction Society's Derringer Award for Best Long Story. It was also selected for the prestigious *Best American Mystery Stories 2018*.

Two dreams come true.

"The Louder the Scream the More Potent the Charm" returned to Africa, the setting for several of my stories (including, of course, "Death in the Serengeti") as well as my novel *No Defense*. It would be the latest fruit borne from my family's trip of a lifetime to Tanzania and Rwanda.

What could possibly go wrong?

Six professional editors, including Kevin, assessed the

story at WMG Publishing's Anthology workshop. The praise I heard was music to my ears.

"The writing was spectacular," said one of the most highly respected writers and editors in the field. "Very powerful.... Kudos to you."

"Well written," said another.

"What a freaking brilliant opening," said a third editor. "Adored it!"

"Hell of a ghost story," said a fourth.

"Helluva story," said a fifth. "Had me all the way through.... Loved it!"

Then came Kevin, the only editor whose opinion truly mattered.

"Unique and fascinating," he said. "Full of great details. Dread. You got me."

My chest swelled with pride.

"But..." Kevin continued.

*You gotta be kidding me.*

My chest, swollen with pride (and the inadvertently held breath that always accompanies these "sentencing hearings" for my stories) deflated like a popped balloon with the words that he wouldn't be buying the story.

So much for the spectacular writing, the freaking brilliant opening, and all the editorial adoration. So much for what I had considered a slam dunk.

Licking my wounds, I submitted the "helluva story" to the top two relevant professional markets. (Not at the same time, of course. In succession.) However, it wasn't a fit for what they were looking for.

By that time, I'd had a chance to think about Kevin's misgivings, and I could see his point. I made structural changes to the second half of the story, submitted the revised version, and got rejected again.

That left one last professional market for which I thought "The Louder the Scream the More Potent the Charm" would be ideal. If it didn't sell there—a magazine I truly loved and read cover to cover every issue—the drop off to the next market would be a steep one. I submitted and held my breath.

And held my breath.

And held my breath some more. Well past the point of passing out.

According to the magazine's website, the story had passed through all the way to the final round of evaluations. Apologies were made for the delay.

So I waited some more. And waited. And waited. After all, this was a market worth waiting for.

Meanwhile, this magazine that had previously published regularly, albeit not frequently, suddenly went a year without a new issue. And then another year. And then another year.

(Coincidentally, I had previously purchased an expensive "lifetime subscription," thinking it would be a bargain unless I prematurely keeled over dead. Um... not a smart move after all.)

The magazine's automated submission tool still said my story was "under consideration." I sent another request for an update.

Crickets.

I suppose it wasn't surprising that a magazine going multiple *years* without a new issue, was keeping new submissions in a permanent holding pattern. The publishing arithmetic was pretty basic. But damned frustrating. So frustrating I wanted to scream (no pun intended). I'd had such high hopes for my "helluva story" (not to mention the extra emotional baggage of that "lifetime subscription" of mine).

Finally, I woke up, smelled the coffee, and choked it down. Black, no sweetener. I withdrew the story from the Magazine From Hell and waited for this collection.

And so I now present to you this "helluva story" that has never appeared anywhere else. You are guaranteed to be reading it for a first time no matter how many magazines you devour.

Despite all the frustrations, I still love it. I hope you will too.

# THE LOUDER THE SCREAM THE MORE POTENT THE CHARM

The ghost streaked through the darkness.

Behind it, the eight men of Nundi pursued, eyes gleaming, sharp knives drawn, machetes at the ready. It would not be long now. They had closed the gap from fifty meters to twenty, racing along the dusty dirt road, the village's sticks-and-mud huts on both sides, the smell of cattle and the day's burning of the fields in the air.

The ghost looked back. It screamed, high pitched and girlish.

Fifteen meters.

Ten.

The ghost raced past the last hut of the village, on the left, the largest and finest of them all, set apart from all others by fifty meters. It was the hut of the healer, Jubutu, the man some called a witch doctor. Jubutu stood outside his front door, tall and slender, almost forty years old, dark arms crossed, watching.

Waiting.

A raging fire burned in a rocky pit twenty meters away from his hut, its crackling flames leaping in the air.

The ghost pleaded. "*Please! Have mercy!*"

But no mercy would be spared on the cursed.

The ghost stumbled and the men were upon it. They slashed their knives and machetes at the ghost's hands and feet, ignoring the thick, red spray, greedily grabbing the slippery rewards of their labors.

The arms and legs came next.

Then its private parts.

Almost nothing was wasted.

The ghost's screams rang loud and shrill, long after its last appendage was severed, guaranteeing that the eight men of the village would prosper.

***

IT WAS late afternoon and Tusa and her mother were alone in their small, circular, sticks-and-mud hut, her father still out in the fields. A fire burned faintly in the center of the floor, surrounded by fist-sized rocks, wisps of smoke curling up to escape through the hole in the roof above. Tonight, the two cloth straps hanging loosely on the walls to both sides of Tusa would be pulled up and tied tight, but for now, light filtered in, providing the hut's only illumination. The air smelled of wood smoke, stale sweat, and perhaps only in Tusa's mind, things best left unspoken.

She sat on her bed, a long, knee-high flat rock to the left of the front door, padded with several layers of cloth.

It was long enough to hold her twelve-year-old body, wide enough for two.

It had felt empty the last three nights. Empty without her twin sister, Kanoni.

Except for the left hand Tusa had lost in an attack two years ago, she and Kanoni had looked identically alike, both albinos with pale, pigmentless eyes, reddish-blonde, closely cropped hair, and skin the lightest milky hue of beige even though they were as African, as Tanzanian, as their dark-skinned mother and father. The twins had always dressed alike. The purple dress with crisscrossed green stripes below the waist that Tusa now wore had its companion hanging in the soft breeze outside.

Tusa knew that she would one day wear it. The family was too poor to throw it away. But not yet.

She still felt her sister's spirit in the hut, and not just because Kanoni's body, what little her attackers had left of it, had been buried at the foot of the bed they'd shared. There was more.

*Tusa, are you there?* Kanoni had asked last night in the silent conversation they had always shared before her death. The question had come while Tusa lay in bed, trying to sleep while Mother wept and Father tried to console her. *Tusa, can you hear me?*

Tusa had answered with a question of her own, the first smile in the last three days forming on her face. *Kanoni?*

But it was a secret Tusa could not share with her mother, who was sitting now on a chair beside the front door, having abandoned any hope of teaching her for the day. Mother taught her at home because Tusa, an accursed ghost, had never been welcome at the schools, could not last outside for long during the day because of the sun's effect on her skin, and more than anything, because it was not safe to step outside their hut. If her own missing left hand hadn't been sufficient evidence, Kanoni's grisly death had eliminated all doubt.

"Will you change my name?" Tusa asked her mother.

Her mother recoiled, as if slapped, and Tusa wondered if she had been cruel to ask. She felt a flash of guilt, but wondered if the jagged edge of the question might have been what Mother needed.

"No, you will always be my Tusajigwe," she said. "No matter what has happened, no matter what will happen, you will always be my Tusa."

"But it means 'we are blessed,'" Tusa said. "How can that be true?"

"I know full well what it means," her mother answered, her voice sharp. "I am the one who told you."

"How can we be blessed when everyone else says that ghosts like us are accursed?"

"Do not call yourself a ghost, Tusa. And you are not accursed."

Tusa almost answered that Kanoni, whose name meant 'little bird,' a sweet little bird whose wings had been broken and devoured alive, had certainly been accursed. But Tusa held back that reply. To have said that most definitely would have been cruel.

"It's time I give you this," Mother said, perhaps awoken from her stupor. She took two steps to the foot of the bed where she and Father slept and withdrew a knife and its sheath. It was the knife Father used to skin animals when he hunted. "Perhaps if I..." Tears pooled in her dark brown eyes and she fell silent for a time.

"Strap this to your leg," Mother finally said. She pulled the knife from its sheath and inspected its sharp edges. "Hide it beneath the folds of your skirt so no one can see it. Tell no one of it, and never, ever use it in anger. Use it only to protect yourself. In case... in case..."

Her hand rose to her mouth. Despair filled her eyes.

***

BURUJI MASSABURI SAT cross-legged on the dirt floor, his back against the wall made of sticks and dried mud, the Nundi witch doctor, Jubutu, standing over him. The midnight darkness was broken only by the flickering flames crackling in the stone-lined pit in the center of Jubutu's expansive hut, a thin plume of smoke drifting up to the hole in the center of the hut's thatched roof. Jubutu smelled of dried blood and dead animals.

Massaburi wasn't used to looking up at anyone. He was a physically imposing man, over two meters tall and with broad, powerful shoulders, the owner and president of Massaburi Mining, the fastest growing mining company in the Mwanza region. He was accustomed to subordinates and strangers alike cowering in his presence. He didn't like craning his neck up at the foul-smelling Jubutu towering over him. He didn't like feeling the sense of unease and foreboding he so readily inspired in others.

But it would be worth it.

Massaburi spat on the still-warm, dead chicken

cupped in his large hands, first its head, crooked atop the neck he'd just broken, then its curved back that seemed to still be trembling, and then its tiny, quivering tail. He shifted the chicken to his right hand, spat upon his already moist palm, then moved it to his left and repeated the process. A log in the fire crackled. The taste of blood, bitter and coppery, filled Massaburi's mouth, though he didn't know why.

There was no explanation other than that he was here with the most powerful witch doctor in the region. He had driven through the dead of night from Mwanza, Tanzania's second largest city, thirty kilometers away, to this tiny village, checking his rear view mirror for a tail, even when he clearly was the only one on the deserted road. He could not afford for his enemies or the people of Mwanza to know that he was here, not when witch doctors had been so recently outlawed.

But it was a risk worth taking.

Massaburi held out the dead chicken to Jubutu, but the witch doctor shook his head.

"Tell the chicken your problems," Jubutu said.

"I have no problems," Massaburi said. "Only wishes."

"Not your brother, dying with the virus?"

Massaburi shivered. "How did you know that?" It was common knowledge among many back in Mwanza that Philippe had AIDS, as did so many others, but how did a witch doctor in such a remote village know such a thing?

But one didn't ask such a question, not to a man such as Jubutu.

"I am not here for my brother."

"A virgin can be found. Sex with her will be his only hope."

"I am not here for my brother," Massaburi repeated. "I am here for myself. For things I wish."

"Tell the chicken. It is your messenger to the spirit, to the jinn."

"I wish to become Lord Mayor of Mwanza," Massaburi began, his neck already growing stiff from having to look up while seated on the dirt floor. "I would be good for the people."

"You would be good for yourself," Jubutu corrected.

"I wish great power," Massaburi conceded. One didn't lie to a witch doctor. "I wish riches beyond which I could ever spend. A long life. And many beautiful women."

The witch doctor smiled, his teeth yellowed and crooked at the corners. "You own a mining company, one named after yourself."

It wasn't a question. Massaburi nodded.

"And you know that a ghost's bones, when mixed to form the proper potion and buried in the ground, will help your mining company find gold."

Again, Massaburi nodded.

"And other parts of the ghost will bless you with great success, even as it was cursed in life. Its private parts will allow you to steal as Lord Mayor and not get caught."

Massaburi swallowed hard. "Yes."

"The danger is great with the new laws and outsiders coming from other lands, trying to tell us what we can and cannot do with those whom the spirits have cursed. But the reward is greater still."

Massaburi felt his heart pounding. This was where the deal would be struck.

"I cannot be seen by anyone other than yourself," he said. "I am prepared to pay fifty thousand dollars provided your men find the albino and harvest it in my absence."

Jubutu remained silent for a very long time.

"Unless you want the weakest *muti*," he finally said, "you will pay one hundred thousand dollars and harvest it with your own hands."

Massaburi gasped. "I can't do that."

"For five thousand dollars, we can get the few bones left behind during a recent harvesting. She was a young ghost, twelve years old, and provided many potent potions. Only a few bones were left behind. Her family, surely one of the most accursed in our land, buried those bones within their hut to prevent grave robbers from stealing what you wish to have. The house is never empty." Jubutu's eyes gleamed and he smiled his crooked-toothed smile. "But there is always a way."

"Then I will—"

Jubutu held up a finger. "Do you really want to settle for a lesser potion? Do you really want only a little more power, a small amount of additional riches, and only a few more women? That is what you will get from the bones of a ghost several days old. The powers of a ghost's body diminish rapidly after death. The best potions are made even while the ghost is dying. In fact, the louder its screams, the more powerful the potion."

Unease washed over Massaburi. He had thought the harvesting would be done by others, no different than that of cattle. But to hear the witch doctor talk of louder screams while he, Buruji Massaburi, performed the harvesting himself—

"There is a girl, the twin of the ghost most recently harvested, that will form a most potent *muti*. Her left hand was taken a year ago, and it showered success on the man who took it. But otherwise she is whole and there is the power of a twin. That power is then multiplied many times over if you harvest her with your own hands.

"You will become rich beyond your wildest dreams. You will find gold wherever your company mines. You will become Lord Mayor of Mwanza, the city second only to Dar es Salaam. But that will only be the beginning. Your destiny is to rule the entire country of Tanzania."

Massaburi's head spun at the thought. First, Prime Minister of Tanzania. And then President. Foreign dignitaries would hang on his every word. Every man, woman, or child in the country would obey his will. He barely heard Jubutu continue, "You will have any woman you desire. Or man or boy or girl." Well, of course, if he was ruling all of Tanzania, he would have all the women of his desires. And he would be rich even if all his mines ran dry.

President Buruji Massaburi.

"Where do we get the girl?" he said.

Jubutu smiled. "You will pay one hundred thousand dollars. Then I will tell you how to get her and bring her to me, still alive."

"Bring her to you? You will not come with me to the harvesting?"

"The harvesting will be done here. I do not go to where a ghost lives."

"I cannot be seen in public dragging the girl here. I am a man of reputation even if word of it does not extend to this village. If I am to pay you one hundred thousand dollars for the *muti*, and I am to harvest it myself, you must be with me, prepared to make the most powerful potion known to man, fresh with the ghost's loudest screams.

Jubutu remained silent for a long time.

Finally, he said, "One hundred twenty thousand."

PITCH BLACK DARKNESS filled the hut, broken only by the glowing embers of the fire in the center of the floor. Tusa lay on her bed—the knee-high, flat rock covered with several layers of cloth beneath her, and one on top, covering her up to her neck.

She did not lay there alone.

Kanoni had returned last night to share it with her, at first nothing more than the faintest of whispers. But she was growing stronger. Tusa still could not see even an outline of her in the bedcovers, nor could she touch her; there was nothing to see or touch. But Tusa sensed the familiar warmth radiating from the other side of the bed. And she smelled once again the faint, almost pleasant scent of Kanoni's sweat.

Kanoni was here. Tusa had heard her last night. She could feel her now. Her other half had returned.

"If only Mother had given you this knife," Tusa whispered, touching the sheath strapped to her leg beneath her bedclothes. "You would still be alive."

"Tusa, be quiet and go to sleep," Father said, lying in bed with Mother on the other side of the hut.

*It wouldn't have helped*, Kanoni said to Tusa, paying Father no mind. *They caught me outside. It was my fault. I was foolish. I thought I could outrun them, but I grew tired. There were too many to fight off.*

"Tusa, be quiet!" Father said.

Tusa's eyes widened. In the silent conversation they had always shared, she whispered soundlessly. *He heard you!*

*I know!*

A smile formed on Tusa's lips just as she sensed one forming on whatever passed as lips for Kanoni. They spoke the next three words in amazement together.

*You're a ghost!*

*I'm a ghost!*

*A real one*, Tusa said to Kanoni. *Not just a cruel word to make us seem less than human. You're really a ghost!*

They began to giggle with delight.

"Tusa, this is your last warning!" Father commanded.

Silence hung in the air.

*Show yourself*, Tusa said in the softest mental whisper she could manage. *Make yourself appear. Don't just talk like a ghost. Look like one!*

The hint of a cloudy mist slowly appeared at the foot of the bed, above where Kanoni had been buried.

HALF AN HOUR LATER, Mother and Father slept, Mother tossing and turning fitfully, Father snoring loudly. Not Tusa. She couldn't sleep, and even if she could, she didn't want to. Not as long as Kanoni, now fully a ghost, was beside her. There was so much to talk about. So many mysteries to understand.

"What does it feel like to be dead?" Tusa finally asked. She'd been unable to speak the words, even in their silent conversation, even though they'd never kept secrets from each other, they'd shared everything. But she couldn't hold back any longer. "And what does it feel like to be dead and then suddenly alive—"

The front door crashed in.

Four men poured into the hut. They raced to Mother and Father's bed. Beat them with metal pipes even as they struggled to get to their feet.

*Get the knife! They're here for you!* Kanoni screamed to Tusa.

Tusa shot her right hand – her only hand – beneath the bedcovers and pulled out the knife that she'd strapped to her leg.

It was too late for her parents. Hard, hollow-sounding raps to their heads had toppled them to the floor, unconscious.

*They'll be okay,* Kanoni said. *But you're next. Get ready with the knife..*

"Clear them out of here," commanded one of the men.

*That's Jubutu, the witch doctor.*

Two of the intruders, formless shapes in the darkness, dragged the parents away, leaving behind two men, the tall, slender shape Kanoni had identified as Jubutu and a more broad-shouldered, powerfully built companion.

"The ghost is over there." Jubutu pointed to Tusa.

A crazy part of Tusa's mind wanted to giggle, point toward where Kanoni's mist-like form had been earlier, and say, "No, the ghost is there."

Instead she gripped the knife and waited. When the large, strong man stepped around the fire in the center of the room and approached, Tusa sprang at him.

She slashed sideways with the knife. It missed the man's throat, but caught a cheek and his nose.

He screamed. "Not my face!"

Tusa slashed again, this time catching his hand, covering his face.

The third slash ripped across the man's throat. A warm spray of fluid – was it really blood? – spurted in Tusa's face.

She wiped it away even as the man gurgled and staggered backward. He staggered forward, then backward. He stepped into the fire and toppled onto the ground.

"You evil, cursed thing!" Jubutu said. "Oh, but I will make you scream." He called out over his shoulder. "You two, get back in here."

*You dare call my sister evil?* Kanoni cried out. *How dare you!*

Jubutu spun about. "Who is that?"

Kanoni's mist-like form began to materialize at the foot of the bed. *I'm the ghost!* she cried. *The ghost come back from the grave!*

Eyes wide, Jubutu stared at Kanoni's shimmering pale image.

Tusa sprang.

She slashed the knife across the witch doctor's throat. He gasped. Tusa cut again.

*I'm the ghost!* Kanoni screamed. *I'm the ghost!*

Even as he choked on his own blood, gurgling, Jubutu couldn't take his eyes off Kanoni.

Tusa slashed across Jubutu's throat. Again and again.

Finally, he crumpled to his knees and fell face forward into the fire.

*I'm the ghost!* Kanoni continued to scream. *I'm the ghost!*

*Enough,* Tusa told her. *There's no one left here to hear you except me.*

But it wasn't quite enough for Kanoni, not until she yelled it many more times.

---

AFTER CHECKING to make sure their attackers were unmistakably dead, the sisters headed for the door to get their parents. Two of the witch doctor's men remained outside, but the head of the beast had been severed. The rest would follow.

"This is the ghost and her sister," Tusa called out from just inside the door. "We've killed Jubutu and his friend. Now we're coming for you."

Tusa stepped back and let Kanoni's misty cloud precede her out the door.

# PEANUT AND THE PENTECOSTAL NUN

# INTRODUCTION TO PEANUT AND THE PENTECOSTAL NUN

I contribute regularly to *Mystery, Crime, and Mayhem.* In fact, I'm part of what editor and publisher Leah Cutter calls her "syndicate." No, that doesn't mean that if any of youze guys ever give the magazine or our books a bad review, you could get whacked... or wake up in bed next to a severed horse's head. (Although nice reviews are always appreciated, *if you know what I mean.* Heh, heh, heh.)

Instead, Leah's "syndicate" of writers all agree to contribute stories to at least two of the four issues released annually. For the most part, I attempt to submit a story for every issue with only one exception. I'm not a fan of cozies, that mystery subgenre that features amateur detectives, no onscreen sex or violence, a slower pace, and a limited cast of characters in a pastoral setting. I prefer my crime fiction to be more hardboiled and gritty, if not outright noir.

However, for this issue's theme of "cozy sidekicks" (such as Watson to Sherlock Holmes), Leah loosened the magazine's usual restriction of no fantastical elements. The sidekick could be, for example, a supernatural "familiar" such as a cat or dog.

I was off and running. I knew just the right sidekick—a fictionalized version of a family Yorkie that is cute as a button and knows it—and the setting—a twist on a camp in Maine where I spent many bliss-filled boyhood summers.

The only question would be whether that Yorkie was the sidekick or the crime-solving star. And that really wasn't a question at all.

The story all but wrote itself.

# PEANUT AND THE PENTECOSTAL NUN

The smell of sizzling cheeseburgers and hot dogs floats lazily from the snack bar through the warm summer evening air. Yellow beams from sodium-vapor lamps mounted thirty feet high and spaced fifty yards apart cut through the darkness. Mosquitos buzz, owls hoot in the distance, and bats dot the darkened sky.

Lines ten and fifteen campers long stretch from the three snack bar windows. The devout campers are still praying back at the tabernacle. These are the degenerates attending Long Lake Pentecostal Camp here in Maine for its swimming, boating, sports, and other recreational activities of the world, and not for saving their eternal souls.

I would still be praying at the altar myself, but someone must oversee these monsters and prevent even the hint of impropriety in their hormone-crazed bodies. Boys are born impure, of course. Every last one of them who gets saved from the clutches of Satan is a miracle.

But girls are born pure and I'm entrusted with the task—with Peanut's help—of keeping them that way. So Peanut and I patrol the hundred yards along the darkened lakefront and dock from the rickety boathouse on the left where all the boys sleep to the twenty cabins on the right that house the girls. It's a thankless and impossible task. Too many teenagers with too many hormones spread out over too many darkened square feet. But we do our best.

The campers smile at Peanut but cringe with fear when they see me. Which is just how I like it. I'm the seventy-year-old, white-haired spinster with piercing eyes behind my granny glasses. I hobble around with a wooden cane that I'm plenty happy to place between a couple that has gotten closer than the approved foot-length apart and have even been known to apply that cane to a misbehaving backside or two. I'll play bad cop to Peanut's good cop if that pries so much as a single soul from the eternal horrors of Hell.

Peanut, my Yorkshire terrier, is a cutie and he knows it. He's worldly as sin and I can't stop him. He doesn't walk, he struts. A bemused, impish smirk seems permanently affixed to his chops. He doesn't have to beg the campers for a morsel of their cheeseburger or hot dog; they offer it without so much of a wagging of his little tail.

In many ways a typical Yorkie, he's all of seven pounds and barely more a foot long with a black coat of fur on his body that turns brown on his head. But beneath that unassuming mop of brown fur lurks the Einstein of Yorkies.

*"You've got that right, sweetie,"* he says to me now.

The first time he spoke to me, not audibly, but in my

mind, I feared demonic possession. Didn't just fear it, actually. I was sure of it. And since no one else could hear his thoughts, that meant that I was the one who was possessed.

A few hundred years back, I'd have been burned as a witch, and rightfully so. But many hours of prayer have shown me that God has granted Peanut and me this gift to do his will. It's not witchcraft at all and I'm no witch.

"*A rationalizaaaaaaation!*" Peanut teases. He glances up at me and his smirk grows even broader.

"Behave!" I mutter under my breath so none of the campers hear me and think I'm just an old bat talking to myself. Already, I'm called the Pentecostal Nun behind my back, which is quite unfair. I may be stricter than any old-time nun who gets joy from rapping the knuckles of children with her ruler, but I'm a Pentecostal Holy Roller, not a Catholic, not a nun. If you ask me, Catholics are all going to Hell, straight to Hell, do not pass Go, do not collect two hundred dollars.

Peanut ignores my command. He doesn't know how to behave. Instead, he struts a few feet ahead of me and wiggles his butt like a scantily clad model on a runway. A harlot.

He waits expectantly for me to catch up. When I do, he sidles up to me.

"*Witches turn me on!*" he says, then starts humping my leg.

Appalled, I say, "Stop it!" a little too loud and kick my leg free. Too late, I look around me to see if anyone has noticed.

Campers in the snack bar line stare at me wide-eyed

as if I really am a witch. It would have been better in their eyes for me to have filled the air with curse words like the heathens on HBO than appear to have kicked the camp's beloved mascot.

"Sister Rebecca!" one of the campers has the audacity to say. She's a thirteen-year-old, skinny Irish redhead with freckles and a name I can't remember. Erin or Shannon or Kellie or something like that. Certainly nothing Biblical. Aghast, she says, "How dare you kick that poor little thing!"

What am I to say? Did these campers staring at me now see Peanut humping my leg? Can I even use words describing it to explain my actions?

Rubbing salt in my wounds, Peanut rolls onto his back and shamefully begins to shake his paws and whimper as if he's been shot.

*"Bad Sister Rebecca!"* he says, mocking me. *"Baaaaad!"*

The Irish girl—Erin, Shannon, Kellie, or whatever her name is—convinces a boy with a hot dog walking by to surrender a morsel and she brings it to Peanut. He wolfs it down, then licks her fingers. Next thing you know, one camper after another is bending their knee to offer him pieces of their hot dog or hamburger.

In many ways, the little attention-hound truly *is* a demon. He decides which rules he'll help me enforce and which he'll ignore. He all but curls up and goes to sleep when I command that he help me find couples breaking the "no physical contact, no closer than a foot apart" rule, unaware that if these hormone-crazed youths are holding hands and putting their arms around each other at the age of thirteen and fourteen, the girls will be pregnant by the time they're eighteen.

But Peanut just yawns at that truism and only pretends to help except in the most extreme cases. He truly has a mind of his own and it certainly isn't the mind of Christ. However, humping my leg and then pretending I've hurt him is a new low.

"I wasn't kicking him," I say to the little monsters. "I was just shaking him off my leg."

They look at me doubtfully. I suppose I shouldn't be surprised at that either. In my day, we respected authority, but these little brats have been spared the rod and thus become totally spoiled.

Just as I begin to shoo them away, Peanut scrambles to his feet. Hackles raised, he looks fervently to his left and then his right.

*"Water! Girl! Drowning!"* he yells into my mind.

And bolts for the dock.

---

I HOBBLE AS BEST I can after Peanut, but he's a blur and I'm an old lady with a cane trying to navigate an uneven grassy surface sloping down toward the lake. In no time, Peanut disappears into the darkness as we leave behind the yellow glow of the sodium lighting. I rush past a few campers—a handful of couples and a few stray boys— who aren't supposed to be here in the dark so close to the water and see the fear and guilt in their eyes. The rule is to stay in the well-lighted areas, but if there's any rule, these monsters will want to break it, and I can guess the additional desires that have led the couples here. I don't even want to think about those unattached boys. There's just too much ground to patrol and too few counsellors.

But that's a battle for another day. I try to memorize the campers' faces as I hobble past them and get to the large wooden dock as fast as I can. Illuminated only by the remnants of the sodium lamps sixty or seventy yards away and the scant moonlight poking through the clouds, the dock is forty feet wide and fifteen feet deep. Wooden benches, painted white like the rest of the dock, run along all three sides except the opening to the lake where campers jump in during recreational hours.

"Help!" an unseen girl cries from the water as I near the dock, her voice barely more than a squeak.

I hear the sound of what I guess to be an arm flailing in the water, then Peanut's roar in my mind of "*Hurry!*"

In the darkness, I can barely make out Peanut springing off the left side bench and dislodging the orange-and-white floatation ring from its hook next to the mailbox where the mail boat pulls up five days a week. The floatation ring and its trailing rope skitters across the dock's surface just as Peanut lands beside it. He skids to a halt, gets behind the ring, noses it to the dock's edge ten feet to the right, then kicks it into the water as hard as his front paw can manage.

"Help!" comes the girl's cry again as I step onto the rear of the dock.

I barely make out the image of the girl in the water before she goes back under.

Peanut leaps into the water toward the orange-and-white floatation ring, landing just short of it, then paddling furiously with his short paws, he noses it toward where the girl was before she went under.

Though I'm a hobbled old lady wearing a gray dress wholly inappropriate for lifesaving, I, too, jump into the water. My dress balloons to the surface, so I pull it down flat against my legs even as the cold water sends shivers up and down my spine.

The girl bobs briefly to the surface almost ten feet away, her head tilted backwards, barely above water, flailing arms outstretched. Terror covers her face.

She reaches for the floatation ring. Touches it with a fingertip. Then slips back under.

I take two swimming strokes toward the girl, kicking off my leaden shoes in the process, then dive beneath the water and wrap my arms around her hips.

I stand on the sandy lake-bottom. It shifts beneath me, what I am sure has been happening to the girl, but I'm still able to lift her to the surface.

Panicking, however, she irrationally reaches down and tries to wrap her arms around me. I'm holding my breath, but I'm no teenager. If this girl persists, she's going to drown us both.

With silent screams of pleading, I beseech my Lord and Savior to rescue us.

*"Push her toward the dock!"* Peanut commands.

I drive my weak legs toward the dock as best I can even as the flailing girl knocks my glasses off. My lungs are about to explode.

And then, miraculously, one of her arms snags the floatation ring. And then the other.

I propel her toward the dock with one last push, then let go and shoot to the water's surface.

I gasp for air.

It comes rushing into my lungs—*thank you, Jesus!*—and I gulp for more even as I hear the girl's choking gasps. In what is surely an answer to prayer, she kicks wildly toward the dock's ladder.

---

I LIFT Peanut onto the dock and he shakes himself dry. The smell of his wet fur fills my nostrils. He sniffs the sobbing, trembling girl as she staggers to the far bench and collapses onto it. Then as clamoring voices approach and I climb up the ladder onto the dock—my dress feeling like it's holding twenty pounds of water—Peanut feverishly sniffs all around the dock, focusing on the edge where the girl apparently fell in.

My hands and legs won't stop shaking. My chest still seems like it's ready to explode. But Peanut pays no attention either to me or the girl. Once again marching to his own drummer, he sniffs his way off the dock and follows his nose up the incline away from the water.

"*She was here with someone,*" he tells me. "*A boy.*"

That's hardly a surprise, but neither me nor the girl are in any condition to do anything about those words or the ones that follow.

"*Find out what happened,*" Peanut says.

Were Peanut to respond to that command himself, it would surely be something sarcastic like, "*That hadn't occurred to me. I'd planned on ordering out for pizza.*" I can all but hear those words in my head. But sarcasm doesn't befit the sanctified soul, so I just nod, gulp a few lungsful of the damp, evening air, and hobble over without my cane to sit down beside the sobbing girl. I wrap my arms around her convulsing body. She smells of worldly perfume and urine, no doubt from peeing herself, but I'm not going to judge.

I have the reputation for being harsh—I've gotten the Pentecostal Nun nickname the old-fashioned way, I've earned it—but not even I am about to interrogate this poor girl in her state. I hold off all the other camp counsellors who've arrived and tell them I'll take care of it as long as they can send the Camp Nurse as soon as possible. They grudgingly walk away and leave us alone.

The girl's name is Mary Chaisson from the Northern part of the state, up in Aroostook county. She's a slender fourteen-year-old with dark black hair, a plain face, and crooked teeth.

"What happened?" I finally ask gently, resting my hand on the girl's.

She averts her eyes and says, "I fell in."

I say nothing.

She adds, "It was an accident."

"What were you doing down here?" I ask, trying to keep my instinctive stern and accusatory tone out of my voice.

She pulls her hand away and puts it in her lap. She shrugs. "I don't know."

"You were here with a boy, weren't you?"

Her body goes rigid, then she shivers. She shakes her head no.

"*His name is Zeke Galasso,*" Peanut says inside my head. "*I tracked him up here to the back of the snack bar. He's the one. The smell is distinctive. I'm sure of it. And he looks, to use your phrase, 'guilty as sin.'*"

I nod in response to Peanut, but Mary Chaisson stares at me as if the nod means I know her denial is untrue.

"Mary, don't make things worse by lying," I say. "You were here with a boy and we both know it. Who was it?"

Her eyes dart this way and that. She looks down at her hands in her lap. So I lay it all out for her.

"It was Zeke Galasso, wasn't it?" I say.

Her eyes pop halfway out of their sockets.

"How could you know that?" she asks. "Oh my God, what they say about you is true! You are a witch!"

I'm not sure whether to grimace or smile. I sure can't explain how I know and I'm not about to lie if I can help it. So I respond with a safe half-truth.

"God knows everything," I say gently.

Her shoulders slump in defeat. She shakes her head sadly. Then the words come out in a torrent.

"Zeke said we should come down here so we could have a little privacy. You know? Get away from you and the other counsellors. I thought he was a nice boy. So we snuck down here and for a while it *was* nice. I mean, I know we broke the rules, but it was nice. I liked it. Especially the kissing. His lips were soft and his tongue tasted of spearmint. It was my first time kissing and it was... sweet."

Mary takes in a deep shuddering breath.

"But then he wanted to do more than that," she says. "I was standing with my back to the water. I guess he'd maneuvered me close to the edge without me realizing it. Then he said that he'd push me in if I wouldn't let him. You know, just joking around. Or at least I thought so. But I got scared because I didn't want to do it and… I can't swim.

"When I told him that, an awful, terrible look came into his eyes. I think it was… the Devil. Zeke told me that I'd better do what he wanted or he'd push me in and I could drown for all he cared. I don't think he really meant it. He was just trying to trick me, but when I tried to get away from him, I tripped and fell in."

Mary shivers and chokes back a sob.

"He just ran away," she says. "Ran away and left me to drown."

———

I pray for Mary, then release her to the Camp Nurse. My glasses and shoes are still in the lake, but someone will fetch them for me tomorrow morning.

Now, I have an appointment with Mr. Zeke Galasso.

And that young man just might have an appointment to meet his maker.

I hobble barefoot, leaning more heavily than usual on my cane, up to the back side of the Snack Bar where Peanut and Zeke Galasso await in the darkness. On the way, I recruit Pastor Luke, the Head Camp Counsellor, to join me. He's half my age with jet black hair, matching glasses, and a sizeable paunch.

Everything is a blur without my glasses, but Peanut spots us as we round the corner.

"*Here he is,*" Peanut says and sidles up to a slender young man sitting on a boulder twice the size of a beach ball.

The young man takes one look at us and bolts for the woods behind him.

Peanut dashes after him, bites into a pant leg, and trips him up. Zeke stumbles to the ground. He rolls over, then jumps back to his feet.

"Zeke, there's no point in running," Pastor Luke says.

Zeke takes two more strides, then Peanut trips him up again.

Zeke lays on the ground, frozen, apparently considering his options. Then with a loud exhalation of air and a slumping of his shoulders, he gives up. He lays his head on the ground and covers his face with both hands.

"Is she okay?" he asks.

"It's a little late to ask that now, young man!" I say.

I march over to him and haul him up by the scruff of the neck. It sends a shooting pain through my hip, but it's worth it. Up close, I can see that he has curly brown hair and is wearing a blue button-down shirt and khakis. I give him a shake. "She could have drowned!"

Peanut growls. "*Is she okay*?" he asks, parroting the question of this vermin.

"She's alive, no thanks to you!" I snap, ostensibly at Zeke, even while answering Peanut, too. "If it were up to me, I'd have you—"

Pastor Luke grasps my hand firmly. It's shaking with righteous indignation. "Maybe I should handle this."

I reluctantly agree.

It takes a scant few minutes for the little demon to

confess. He claims that he never would have pushed Mary in.

"I was just seeing if I could get her to do what I was sure she wanted to do anyway," Zeke says.

"*If only I were a Rottweiler,*" Peanut says, and for once, he and I agree.

Pastor Luke calls the police first and then Zeke's parents. He tells the parents that if the police won't take their son off his hands, they'd better make the two-hour drive and do it themselves.

No longer needed here, I leave and hobble barefoot toward my designated cabin, with Peanut trotting along by my side. It's only a few minutes away from Lights Out, so my eight girls had better be back in the cabin and tucked in their bunk beds. I suspect every last one of them will be. They're all well behaved.

At least they are now. I wonder, though, how long it will be before one of them falls into the clutches of an evil boy like Zeke.

"What's wrong with the male gender?" I ask Peanut, shaking my head in disgust. "Most of you are headed straight to Hell. Present company excepted, of course."

Peanut wastes no time in responding.

"*What's wrong with you humans?*" he fires back. "*Most of you are headed straight to Hell. Present company excepted, of course.*"

I stop and stare at him. "If you weren't a dog, I'd have to pray for you."

His ever-present smirk seems to grow even more pronounced.

"*And if you weren't the Pentecostal Nun,*" he says, "*I'd have to pray for you, too.*"

He scampers a few feet ahead, then wiggles his behind.

I shake my head in exasperation, but the unfamiliar feeling of a smile slowly creeps over my face.

# BUBBA AND THE DELOREAN

# INTRODUCTION TO BUBBA AND THE DELOREAN

Bubba Winslow came into my world after I completed my first novel, *Cracking the Ice*, a Young Adult sports novel set in 1968 at the height of the Civil Rights struggle. The novel's protagonist, a Black phenom hockey player named Jessie Stackhouse, leaves home to break the color line at an elite, all-white prep school. He arrives filled with dreams of winning championships and eventually playing in the NHL but soon finds that the coach doesn't want him there and neither do most of his teammates.

The New York editor who bought *Cracking the Ice* considered it an "important" book. A number of major writers who provided their endorsements agreed. *Booklist* said, "Hendrickson's debut novel paints a gripping account of a courageous young man rising above evil." (I'm likely to get that quote plastered on my tombstone. I've certainly made sure it's appeared almost everywhere else.) Another reviewer called it "a one-of-a-kind book."

Wow.

Important! *Important!* **Important!**

After finishing *Cracking the Ice* (and before much of the fanfare that developed), my creative subconscious decided it needed a break from *important* and so it created Bubba Winslow, the world's dumbest crook. He would "star" in my next novel, *Bubba Goes for Broke.* Talk about going from one end of the spectrum to the other. With an abundance of lowbrow humor, *Bubba Goes for Broke* couldn't possibly have been any less important. Just fun.

My New York editor was aghast at the whole thing. *Cracking the Ice* was Young Adult-genre squeaky clean; *Bubba Goes for Broke* dropped an F bomb in the opening paragraph and continued with R-rated humor (think *Two and a Half Men*). She told me in no uncertain terms that not only did she not want *Bubba* as the follow-up book to which she held an option—*quelle surprise!*—but I had damned well bury it under a pseudonym. I was happy to do so and was already at work writing a suitable Young Adult title for her. The pseudonym I chose was David H. Bawdy (rather descriptive I thought), and the YA title would become *Offside.*

A few other New York publishers liked *Bubba Goes for Broke*, but it didn't quite fit for them. Traditional publishing was also undergoing the Kindle-inspired revolution I've mentioned in previous introductions, so *Bubba Goes for Broke* became my first independently published (aka "indie") novel. As a result, Bubba, loveable galoot that he is (well, sort of lovable), earned a special place in my heart.

He resides there still.

I employ only a few ongoing series characters, but when it comes to humor, Bubba tops the list. In fact, he *is* the list.

So it was quite natural during a workshop combining humor and science fiction that Bubba came riding to my rescue. And, of course, since it was science fiction, he came riding in a DeLorean. A very special DeLorean, of course. When it comes to science fiction, is there any other kind?

Writing "Bubba and the DeLorean" was a ton of fun, and Dean Wesley Smith felt the same way about reading it. He bought it for *Pulphouse Fiction Magazine*.

All of which has convinced me that having a ton of fun, even lowbrow humor fun, is in its own way important as hell.

# BUBBA AND THE DELOREAN

It was the perfect day to steal a car. The sun beat down from a cloudless sky, but a cooling breeze made the early June day quite pleasurable. The half-full parking lot outside of the MIT Advanced Physics Laboratory smelled of recently applied asphalt, its smooth, black surface marred only by a handful of stains from leaking antifreeze, oil, and gasoline.

But for Bubba Winslow, every day was a perfect day to steal a car. He'd been stealing cars since he was a teenager. It was the one thing in life he did best, followed closely, of course, by romancing the ladies, who loved his 6-3, 210-pound, chiseled physique and his thick, jet black hair. Not to mention the prodigious endowment he liked to call the Big Bubba Meat Stick. But pleasuring women didn't pay the bills, though he'd been wondering lately if he should start charging. Stealing cars paid the bills.

So Bubba snuck from one possible target in the lot to the next, the tools of his trade tucked inside his black leather jacket. There were about fifty cars in the square-shaped lot, most of them worth stealing, but his eyes were drawn to a fenced-in, canopied area up against the brick building that housed only a single car, hidden in the shadows.

If it was fenced in, Bubba reasoned, the car had to be valuable. He knew he wasn't the smartest guy out there—he'd have dropped out of kindergarten if that had been allowed—but he wasn't as bad as everyone else said, especially The Boss, who called him the "second or third dumbest crook in the universe."

Not even in the Top Ten, Bubba was quite sure. And spotting the fenced-in car would be Exhibit A.

When he got close, Bubba saw that it was a classic silver DeLorean, the car whose doors swung up not out. Like in the movies. Not at all what he was looking for but a sweet payday. And fifteen-foot-high fencing spelled extra dollar signs for Bubba. He could even see now barbed wire atop the fencing, hidden beneath the canopy, and a Danger sign with a skull and crossbones on it just below the barbed wire.

Big dollar signs.

Checking to make sure the coast was clear, Bubba pulled his tool kit from beneath his black leather jacket, and in less than three minutes he'd cut through the fence, broken into the DeLorean, and hot-wired the ignition.

Only then did he realize there was no way he could drive the DeLorean anywhere. It was still caged inside the fifteen-foot-high fence.

Now didn't that suck. And instead of being Exhibit A for his unappreciated brain power, it had become Exhibit

A for him being, sad to say, the second or third dumbest crook in the universe.

*I are a moron*, he thought.

Then things got worse.

A recessed door in the abutting brick building swung open and a *fine*-looking, petite Japanese woman with professorial black-rimmed glasses rushed out.

"What are you doing?" she shrieked. "Don't touch anything! It's dangerous!"

Bubba looked at the control panel to see what could possibly be dangerous if he touched it. Anytime he saw a sign that said Wet Paint, he couldn't stop himself from testing it, and this woman's panicked warning of danger just screamed Wet Paint to him. But the panel was just a bunch of knobs, highlighted by a big black one in easy arm's reach, and buttons that meant nothing to him.

Before he could try any of them, the woman pulled up the DeLorean's driver-side door and leaned in.

"Get out of there!" she yelled. "Now!"

"Why?" Bubba asked.

"It's a very dangerous, experimental device. It could kill you."

"What kind of a device?"

"I can't tell you," the woman said. "Please! You should leave right now. Security is on the way."

"In that case—" Bubba said, and reached for a large black knob.

"No!" the woman yelled.

"Tell me what it does," Bubba insisted, his hand back in his lap. "Or I'll just keep twisting knobs and find out for myself. If I'm about to get arrested, I've got nothing to lose."

The woman blinked, then swallowed hard.

Bubba reached for the large knob.

"It's a time machine," she finally said.

"Come on!" Bubba said. She was treating him like he was an idiot.

"No, really!"

"Like in the movies?"

"It can only go back in time. Not forward, not even a nanosecond. But anywhere back in time, even to mythical places that never really existed. But it's likely to kill you in the process. It's highly experimental and top secret."

"If it's top secret, why have it out here in the open?"

"What better way to hide it?"

Bubba thought about what he'd seen in movies about time travel, then considered the two things he cared the most about: money and sex.

"So I could go back in time and find out about the stock market or sports or horses, then come back to the current time and buy stocks and place huge bets that are guaranteed winners."

The woman rolled her eyes and shook her head.

"First off, the machine would probably kill you," she said. "So far, we've only experimented on mice and the fatality rate is over ninety percent. And you can't bring anything back. Not money or any assets. Only knowledge about your experience in the past."

"But there's a ten percent chance I survive, come back, and use those guaranteed winners to become the richest man alive."

"Less than ten percent of the mice survive. A human's odds would be much, much worse."

Bubba still liked his chances. The richest man alive. How sweet that would be! Certainly worth the risk.

The woman looked at him as if he were an idiot. A look he got all the time.

"If you survived," she said, "you could come back here knowing every racehorse and sports team that ever won and every corporate stock that ever made millions, but what good would it do?"

"I'd become the richest man alive!" Bubba said, marveling at the woman's failure to comprehend the obvious.

"You can't bet on a race or sports event that happened ten years ago," she said. "Everyone already knows who won it! The same thing with stocks!"

Bubba blinked, letting it all sink in. The dollar bills the had been floating around in his head suddenly disappeared.

"Oh yeah," he said.

Silence fell and stretched for what felt like forever.

"So what good is the damned thing?" Bubba asked.

"Eventually, we hope to go back and learn about the past."

"So I could turn that knob and if I turned it all the way, I could go all the way back to the Garden of Eden?"

"Theoretically, yes, if it didn't kill you," she said. "That would be the mythical past I referred to. Unless, of course, you believe Adam and Eve actually existed."

Bubba thought back to his days in Catholic school. He hadn't been to church in decades, but he recalled the teaching that Adam and Eve had walked around the Garden of Eden naked.

Bubba was willing to bet Eve was one fine-looking woman.

Perpetually naked.

Suddenly, police burst through the building door, guns pointed. The woman stepped back from the car and pointed at him. Too late, Bubba realized the woman had been telling him all this—talking up a storm and who knew how much of it was total nonsense—just to stall until the cops arrived.

With nothing to lose, Bubba reached out and turned the big, black knob counterclockwise all the way.

*Eve,* he thought, *you'd better be good looking. And Adam, she ain't never gonna be looking at you the same way again! There ain't no fig leaf that can cover up the Big Bubba Meat Stick!*

---

BUBBA WAS PONDERING his member perpetually at full attention in the Garden of Eden—where Eve would no doubt be throwing herself at him with his sculpted body and prodigious endowment—when he fell from the sky and landed in a thicket of bushes and overgrown weeds.

For several seconds, Bubba just lay there, looking up at the cloudless sky. Where was he? Was this the Garden of Eden? It sure didn't smell like it. The stench of what was almost certainly manure filled the air.

Bubba got to his feet and brushed the tangled weeds and brambles off his jeans and black leather jacket. He took a comb out of his back jeans pocket and pulled it through his hair. If Eve was out there, gorgeous and deliciously naked and looking to party, he had to look his best.

Finally, he surveyed the scene. Behind him and off to the sides were thick woods for as far as the eye could see. Before him were vast fields being plowed by a half dozen men and their oxen. Or at least that's what Bubba thought they were doing. He didn't know much about farming. But he'd certainly been right about the manure.

This was no Garden of Eden. And there was no DeLorean in sight to make an exit from this smelly hellhole.

"I've done it again," Bubba muttered.

He supposed he could ask the men in the field for help, but he figured that was almost certain to backfire. If they even understood his language, could they ever comprehend what he told them?

*I'm from the future. A DeLorean time machine. Think you could help me get back home?*

Yeah, like that would work.

And what skills could he offer them to avoid being killed on sight? *I steal cars and pleasure women.*

Women. Bubba blinked as that pleasant idea formed in his head. Yeah, women. Now *that* would be moving in the right direction.

He scanned the horizon and spotted two clouds of smoke in the distance. Cooking, perhaps? He doubted women were liberated here in the most ancient of times. They certainly weren't out here plowing the fields.

Slowly, staying out of sight of the men, Bubba began

circling around the fields, working his way toward the clouds of smoke.

———

THE WOMAN COOKING something that smelled delicious over a crackling fire looked positively delicious herself. Dark brown animal skins barely covered her private parts. A lot like, Bubba thought, an ancient version of a string bikini up top and a thong down low. A golden tan covered the rest of her body. This raven-haired beauty would look mighty fine in a *Sports Illustrated* swimsuit issue.

Perhaps missing out on the Garden of Eden wasn't that big a tragedy after all.

Bubba slipped out from the woods and walked confidently toward the woman. He flashed his most winsome smile and held his arms out to show that he meant no harm.

"Hello, my name is Bubba," he said, though somehow the words he heard in his ears sounded quite different from what he spoke with his lips. Some kind of time-travel automatic translation? It had to be something like that. He continued, "I'm from the future. Just like in the movies."

The beautiful woman cocked her head and frowned, clearly not understanding a word.

"*I'm from the future!*" Bubba bellowed at close to maximum volume. "*Just like in the movies!*"

"There's no need to holler," the woman said, albeit with the movement of her lips not matching the words as if this were an old Godzilla movie. Had to be an automatic translator. "But what do you mean 'from the future?' I don't understand. And what's a movie?"

That stopped Bubba in his tracks. He had no idea how to explain what a movie was, much less the concept of the future.

He just stared.

"What are those clothes you wear?" the woman asked, and walked slowly to him.

Bubba grinned with pride. "These tight-ass jeans and T-shirt are Calvin Kleins. Nike sneakers. And my leather jacket is by Armani."

"Who are these... Calvin Klein, Nike, and Armani?" the woman asked, looking confused.

"The best," Bubba said. "Only the best." He nodded with satisfaction. "Me and Calvin are really tight."

The woman reached out and stroked the black leather jacket with fascination.

"I've never felt anything like it!" she purred.

Every stroke of the jacket seemed more and more sexual. At least it was for Bubba. *Oooh baby.*

Barely able to think straight with the raven-haired beauty stroking his jacket, Bubba asked, "What is your name?"

"Saundra," she replied.

"*Saundra,*" Bubba said, barely suppressing a moan. "A beautiful name befitting your beauty."

"Who are you?" Saundra asked.

"I'm Bubba. Bubba Winslow."

She took Bubba's right hand, lifted it, and sniffed the jacket at the cuff. Her eyes widened, either at the leather smell or the scent of his cologne he always applied to both wrists.

"Where do you come from?" she asked, clearly mystified at the magic that was Bubba.

"The future," Bubba said, knowing that wasn't helping at all, but so intoxicated by the woman that he was unable to think of anything more useful.

"You keep saying that, but I know of no such land."

"It's... it's far, far away," Bubba said.

"I don't understand," Saundra said. "Are you not also a descendant, as are we all, of our father and mother, Adam and Eve?"

"I suppose so," Bubba said. "That's what the nuns said."

"Who are the nuns?" Saundra asked and shook her head, looking totally bewildered.

Bubba realized he'd stepped in it again. He opened his mouth to reply, then closed it. There was no way he could ever explain the concept of a nun.

Saundra frowned. "Your father is not Adam and your mother is not Eve? How can that be? Since they were cast out of the Garden, there have only been my ten brothers, my fifteen sisters, and me. And the three small children borne by three of my sisters. I have never heard of you. How can you even exist?"

Bubba let that all sink in.

"You're telling me that until I showed up," he said, "there were only your parents, Adam and Eve, and their ten sons and sixteen daughters plus the three small children."

"Yes, of course. You are a mystery. Are you an angel?"

"Ten of your brothers are married to ten of your sisters?" Bubba asked, inwardly wincing at the idea of incest.

"Of course. We are the only humans on Earth. Until you showed up."

"You are not married?" Bubba said, his heart beginning to pound. "And that is also the case for five of your sisters?"

"That is true," she said, looking downcast. "We must wait until our sisters' male offspring come of age."

"Your wait is over," Bubba said, spreading his arms and beaming. Pulling up old memories from Catechism, he said, "Your mother and father were told to be fruitful and multiply. I'm the answer to your prayers!"

---

Bubba wasn't sure if there was a possible way to get back to his own time. But if there was, he didn't want it.

He convinced Saundra and her five unwed sisters that future generations for thousands of years would allow men to take many wives, and even more importantly, that he offered far more to all six of them than either their gross and disgusting brothers or nephews they would have to wait for during the prime of their own lives. He was the man for all six women.

Like a thoroughbred racehorse, Bubba put himself out to stud.

# THE OTHER SIDE OF THE TRACKS

# INTRODUCTION TO THE OTHER SIDE OF THE TRACKS

An anthology is a collection of stories by different writers, compiled by an editor, and released as a single book. An "uncollected anthology," therefore, makes no sense. It's an oxymoron. How can it be an anthology if the stories aren't collected?

The Uncollected Anthology, however, is an outstanding ongoing series of urban and contemporary fantasy stories, released three times a year at an agreed-upon date on an agreed-upon theme by a group of terrific writers who release their stories independently. Uncollected.

The oxymoron works. Wonderfully.

Of course, writers being what we are—controlling us is like trying to herd cats—that single oxymoron wasn't enough. The Uncollected Anthology writers decided to double down. They would not only coordinate the simultaneous release of their individual stories but also... get this... *collect them* into a single book.

In other words, *collect* the stories in the *Uncollected Anthology.* A double oxymoron.

Hey, these are some of the most brilliant writers on the planet, so who am I to nitpick over one total contradiction layered on top of another? And when they asked me to be a guest author in their *Conjuring Crime* issue, well, I signed up for the double oxymoron with enthusiasm, and for once in my life kept my big mouth shut. After all, I'm a bastion of inconsistencies and contradictions myself.

An honor is an honor is an honor. And of course, it's the story that matters, not the mechanics of its release, no matter how wonderfully unique.

I was delighted with the end result. I'd like to think "The Other Side of the Tracks" is a quintessential merging of crime and fantasy. Double the fun. And quite appropriate to have first appeared in a double oxymoron publication.

# THE OTHER SIDE OF THE TRACKS

Patrol cars block off the empty street, their blue strobe lights pulsing through the midnight darkness, yellow crime scene tape cordoning off the two blocks to the train station. Overhead, streetlights cast their hazy, eerie orange glow. The sidewalk, stained with pigeon droppings and littered with crumpled paper bags and coffee cups, smells of urine, feces, and blood. A sour taste floods my mouth and the back of my throat. My knees pop and my suit jacket flares out as I crouch down for a closer look.

Pointing the beam of my heavy-duty flashlight on her face, I stare at the ghastly remains of Katrina Miller. In life, she was anything but pretty. She had the rotted teeth and acne-riddled face of a meth head. Distant, sad brown eyes. Tangled, black hair that hung limply to her shoulders. An emaciated figure, little more than skin and bones.

But now... ghastly.

I fight back the instinctive rumblings in my gut as I take pictures with my phone. Never in my two decades on the Bleektown Police Force—hard decades on our city's mean streets that ended both of my marriages, turned my hair gray with streaks of premature white, and put me on high dosages of blood pressure medication despite my scrawny build—have I seen anything like this. And I've seen a lot in this fucking cesspool.

Katrina's face, arms, and back have been shredded, carved into inch-wide ribbons. Fist-sized chunks of her neck and shoulders have been ripped out. Her blood has been sopped up somehow though it still stains the sidewalk beneath her. Sopped up, or perhaps, revolting as the idea may be, lapped up.

I try to piece it together and instinctively suspect that the sick fuck who did this worked with a very large attack dog at least the size of a full-grown German shepherd, if not larger. I can even smell the scent of dog in the air. It sank its sharp teeth into Katrina's neck and shoulders and feasted on the flesh and muscle before lapping up her blood. Then it walked away, leaving bloody paw prints all the way to the far side of the commuter train station two blocks away where they suddenly disappear. I wonder if perhaps that's where it jumped into the murderer's car, and together they sped off, their carnage complete.

At least that's my initial theory. And it points to Clint Parish, Katrina's pimp. Who owns a large German shepherd. Cute name of Killer.

Katrina worked the streets of this city, an hour north of Boston. Tight black miniskirt on an anorexic body and heels. Eighteen going on eighty. Assholes would pull their car up to her on this corner—her corner—roll down the window, and ask the price. She'd quote a number. Maybe the asshole would try to negotiate or ask about her willingness to indulge some sick desire. Then she'd climb in.

She almost always climbed in. I figured that would be her demise if the meth didn't kill her first.

But she didn't climb in this time. This time, for some reason, a sick fuck and his dog came after her.

Clint Fucking Parish.

But I can't jump to conclusions. Detective Principles 101. I can't fall into the classic trap of developing tunnel vision in a case before all the evidence is in. And the evidence hasn't even been collected yet. Gloved up, I use tweezers to pick up what looks like a gray dog hair, if not for its too-long length of almost five inches, and put it in an evidence bag. Although the late August air is heavy with no wind, I'm taking no chances of it blowing away while I wait for Tompkins, our Crime Scene Investigator, to arrive. There are another couple hairs stuck to blood on the sidewalk, but I leave them for Tompkins. They ain't going anywhere.

I straighten up, knees popping yet again, and scan the area.

Other than four patrolmen and two other detectives, the streets are empty. The other prostitutes and the drug dealers who sell their wares and their souls in this part of downtown have long since disappeared, evaporating into the bleak darkness. And theirs are the only downtown businesses usually open this late. Behind Katrina's body is the boarded-up storefront of a once-proud hardware store, now covered with crude graffiti. To the left and right are other boarded-up businesses, symbols of a downtown as dead as Katrina: a former clothing store, pizza place, and Mom-and-Pop pharmacy. Only a Dunkin Donuts remains in business, propped up by commuters using the train station a couple blocks away, but even the Dunks closes at ten, the foot traffic from the final train out of Boston insufficient to stay open, the whores and the dealers unwelcome customers.

"Anyone see anything?" I ask a young Vietnamese detective named Linh Nguyen, who's been hovering with her partner on the periphery behind me. She's short and thin, but with strong-looking shoulders, her long, black hair tied back.

"A patrol car was first on the scene, but we were right behind," interrupts her partner, Tom Jenkins. Middle-aged, beefy, florid, sandy-haired. "Wasn't a soul in sight. Even the damned whores and dealers were gone."

"You touch anything?" I ask, an edge in my voice.

"Of course not," Jenkins replies, then adds in a tone laced with sarcasm. "You're the great Senior Detective Jack McTavish. Tarnish his crime scene and he'll ream you a new one."

"Good to hear the word's out," I say. "Who called it in?"

"Anonymous tip," Jenkins says. "Came in seconds after midnight. Sounded mostly like a female, according to the desk, but with a husky, almost masculine tone. No accent."

"Mostly female, but almost masculine? What the fuck does that mean?" I ask.

"Could be trying to disguise his or her voice," Nguyen says. "Or a Non-binary. We'll be able to listen to the recording. They're tracing the number, but my guess is a burner."

Jenkins looks at her acidly, as if to ask who the hell she thinks she is. He yanks a thumb in her direction and mutters, "The rookie's bucking for a promotion."

I can't see if she flushes in the streetlight's orange glow, but she does purse her lips.

"No one was here at all when you arrived?" I ask.

"No," she says, shaking her head.

"That's what I said," Jenkins says. "Unless you count the body."

I shake my head. *Asshole.*

"How long before the M.E. arrives?"

"He's on his way," Jenkins says.

"About fifteen minutes," Nguyen says.

"How about Tompkins?" I ask. As our Crime Scene Investigator, he'll collect the blood samples, the hairs embedded in the blood, and other DNA and possible fingerprint evidence.

"Same," Jenkins says.

"Okay, you two fan out that way," I say, pointing to our left, away from the train station. "See if you spot anything or anyone. The blues will keep the crime scene secure. I'll go the other way and check it out again. If I'm not around when you're done, find out her last known address. Get going on a search warrant. See if there's any next of kin."

The paw prints lead me all the way to the far side of

the train station, growing less distinct but still visible every ten yards or so, a sick testament to just how much blood was spilt. I take photographs as I go and also a few impressions onto fingerprint pads, which I bag and seal. The bloody prints go around the single set of twenty-one stairs that lead to the enclosed, elevated platform from which inbound trains arrive on one side and outbound on the other. Instead, the prints continue on the asphalt past the station entrance to the other side of the tracks. There, they stop suddenly up against the thirty-foot-high, hundred-foot-long, graffiti-covered rock face that makes up the station's back side and borders its small, barely used parking lot.

Oddly, the final paw prints *face* the rock wall instead of the now-empty, fifty-car lot, where I would have expected the savage animal to have climbed into the murderer's car. But it couldn't have climbed in a car while facing the wall. So, what was it doing? This wasn't a little Chihuahua or Yorkie that could have been picked up by its owner. This was a huge dog. A beast. Only a weightlifter could have hoisted it. And why?

I take more photographs, noting that the final bloody paw prints face a specific section of graffiti that features the side view of a six-foot high yellow dragon with vivid blue eyes and a red tongue. It's breathing out a huge orange flame. Not quite professional artwork but extraordinary for graffiti. Of course, since nothing of beauty must be allowed to stand in Bleektown, some asshole has covered the dragon's colorful torso with three words in crude black spray paint:

# JoJo

+

# Paul

I look for tire tracks or any other evidence in the closest parking spots, but there's nothing but old oil stains and weeds poking out of the cracks in the asphalt. I take one last look at the rock wall, trying to imagine the huge dog staring at the dragon, its bloody snout inches away, blood still staining its paws, and then getting lifted cleanly without so much as a smudge to the prints or a shoe print of whoever could lift such a beast.

I shiver despite the August heat and humidity. I've always found the wall unsettling in some instinctive way I can't understand or put into words. Not because of the offensive phrases that appear on a regular basis, must be spray-painted over by the DPW, and then reappear almost instantly again. There's no rational reason at all for my discomfort.

When you see the things I see in this cesspool of a city, it makes no sense for a fucking rock wall to give you goose bumps and make the hairs on your arms stand up as if the damned thing is electrified. What's truly disturbing is what's done to the Katrina Millers of the world every day of the week. But there's no denying my instinctive, wholly irrational reaction to the place.

I slowly head back to the crime scene, looking for something I might have missed on my way over here but finding nothing. Not for the first time, I'm grateful that the city's longstanding newspaper, *The Bleektown Beacon*, bit the dust four years ago. Cases like this are ugly enough without having to shoo off a nosy journalist and photographer. And the Boston papers rarely sully themselves with Bleektown news. Murders in Bleektown aren't news. They're par for the fucking course. And murders of whores even more beneath consideration.

My rage builds as I reflect on that attitude, one shared by many of Bleektown's alleged upstanding citizens. The death of a whore doesn't count. Addition by subtraction. Part of a needed cleansing process.

Well fuck them.

Katrina Miller was a human being whose life had value, even if she wasn't long for this world. I never found out what led to her self-destructive choices. She always rebuffed my attempts at conversation even when we were alone with no chance of her pimp or other prostitutes observing us. And the few times I questioned her, trying to get some lead on a case, she'd only say, "I don't know nothing."

There was no getting to her. No getting through the impenetrable wall she set up. No saving her.

All I can do for her now is seek justice. Find the sick fuck who did this to her and make him pay.

Suspect Number One is Clint Fucking Parish.

It's almost two in the morning before I finally leave the crime scene for Clint Parish's house on the other side of town, what feels like another universe. It's a residential area consisting of tract houses with cookie cutter lawns, fences, and driveways. A neighborhood that likes to pretend that downtown and the likes of Katrina Miller don't exist, and the grisly death of a whore is nothing more than the wages of sin. Its children go to parochial schools or even some lower-level private ones to avoid the rundown and sometimes violent public schools populated by the detritus from the Bleektown's "other" neighborhoods.

A streetlight's glow casts an orange tint on Clint Parish's white, two-story house at the far-right end of this dead-end street. I pull up to the curb, alone as usual, and call in my position. Sometimes I'm paired for a few shifts with Nguyen or Jenkins in what are termed "training sessions," and Jenkins invariably mutters sarcastically about "learning from the master." But when the shit hits the fan, I don't want them slowing me down. Especially Jenkins.

And the shit has hit the fan.

They'll be dispatched to this address if I don't report back in a designated amount of time as a safety measure, but for now I'm on my own. I don't immediately disrupt the peace by heading to Clint's front door and banging the shit out of it. Not out of respect for the time of night or for any one of the assholes on this street and certainly not for him.

Instead, from my position on the edge of the street, I focus my flashlight's powerful beam on the asphalt, bending down for a better look. I use my phone to take pictures then use my tweezers to capture and bag what are likely—since this is the end of a dead-end street—the gray hairs from Killer, Clint's German shepherd. I photograph the paw prints on the road's sandy shoulder just before the grass of Clint's lawn begins, then moisten the paw prints with my spit and take impressions on fingerprint pads. The street is public domain, and I don't need a search warrant to keep this evidence legit like I would from his lawn or house.

Soon, though, my heart isn't in it. I walk slowly along the asphalt walkway to Clint's front door, visually comparing the paw prints embedded in the lawn with those I've just taken. As best I can tell, they're a match, though I'd need a warrant to collect evidence from the lawn to be sure. But the hairs are no match for the much longer and more coarse hairs I saw downtown and the paws are barely half the required size to match with the claws no match at all.

Which blows a king-sized hole in my theory. Perhaps, these prints and hairs are from another dog from the area or Clint owns more than one of them. But though my theory is already in tatters, my hatred for Clint remains. Too bad that isn't sufficient for me to arrest him.

I mount the four brick steps to the ten-by-ten front porch, ring the doorbell, and bang the shit out of the white pine door.

After a minute or two, an overhead porch light comes on and Clint's raspy snarl erupts from the other side.

"What the fuck do you think you're doing, McTavish?" he yells, no doubt seeing my ugly mug through his peephole. "It's two o'fucking clock in the morning!"

Though the door remains closed and the peephole works only from the inside out, I see him clearly in my mind. Thirty-eight years old. Pale white skin. Six-two, two-sixty with a good fifty of those pounds in a pronounced beer belly. Rust-colored, tangled hair hanging down to his broad shoulders. Imitation jailhouse tats on his biceps. No one has actually been able to put him away, but he likes them for show.

"I need to talk to you, Clint."

"'bout what?"

"Open the door and we'll talk."

"You got a search warrant?"

"Not yet."

"Then fuck off!"

Killer, Clint's German shepherd, growls loudly as if on cue.

"It might be better for you if you talk to me now," I say.

"It might be better for you if you kiss my ass."

"Hey, I know you don't want me to come in and see all the illegal shit you got," I say. "So just come out and we'll talk." I add casually, "Bring the dog. I don't care."

"Talk to my lawyer."

"Where were you tonight?"

"Talk to my lawyer."

I consider saving my questions for if and when I get a search warrant. But I don't like my chances of getting one based purely on my knowledge that that Clint is Katrina's pimp. *Was* her pimp. The department long ago gave up on prostitution arrests except for the months leading up to the local elections. As a result, there's no documentation officially linking him with Katrina.

So, I decide to show my cards. If Clint killed her, he already knows why I'm here.

"Just tell me when you last saw Katrina Miller. She's one of your girls, right?"

I hear a muffled conversation on the other side of the door. Clint and what sounds like a female voice.

"Is that her you're talking to?" I ask, knowing full well the answer.

"Why you asking about Katrina?" Clint asks.

"Is that her you were just talking to?"

"Yeah, it is," he says. "Now go away and let me sleep."

"You were just talking to Katrina?" I say matter-of-factly. "Really? That's funny, her body's in the morgue."

A shriek erupts from inside. Muffled words that sound like "her too?" Then a hard slap and a body—the woman, I'm sure—crashes to the floor. She begins to cry.

Clint, asshole that he is, has just now given me all I need to force my way inside without a warrant. Exigent circumstances. The health and well-being of the woman are at immediate risk. And that's besides her muffled words. If I heard them right—"*Her, too?*"—they send shivers down my spine.

I'm pretty damned sure I heard them right.

*Her, too?*

"I'm coming in, Clint!" I yell, and crash the side of my body into the door. It doesn't budge. Of course. It's got to be triple dead bolted.

I draw my weapon, a Glock 22, from the shoulder holster inside my jacket. I hold it against the small of my back. A sour taste floods the back of my mouth and throat. Pain stabs my eyeballs.

"Step back! Both of you!" I yell. "I'm blowing the lock off! Get back! I'm not standing out here while you beat the shit out of that woman. I'm coming in!"

"Stop!" Clint yells. "Don't shoot! Don't shoot!"

I wait.

"I'll come out." Clint says, then repeats himself. "I'll come out."

But there's only silence except for Killer growling. That and the pounding of my heart in my eardrums.

"I'm waiting," I finally say. "You got five seconds, Clint."

"Put your gun down," he says. "I ain't coming out just to get shot."

"I'll put the gun down," I say, "when I see your empty hands."

"I got no weapon on me," he says. "I'll show you my hands. But Sheila here is gonna record everything through the doorway. You lay one finger on me and it'll all be on video. Not just on the phone, in case you try to grab it, but in the fucking Cloud. And Killer's coming out with me, too. You try anything, he'll rip your fucking throat out."

"Sheila comes out, too," I say. "I need to see that she's safe."

"Sheila stays right the fuck where she is," Clint says right back. "Recording everything. Keeping you honest. You'll see she's plenty safe."

It seems the best I can do. I back to the far edge of the porch, almost on the first step down, ten feet from the door.

"Okay, come on out. Slowly," I say. "Hands out where I can see them. Don't make me do something we both don't want."

"You ain't arresting me, right? Cause I ain't done nothing. We just talking, right? Like you said."

"Yeah, just talking. So long as I can see that the woman inside—Sheila—is all right."

The door opens a crack. Killer pokes its nose out and growls, its sharp, white fangs bared. Then its whole head emerges through the widening doorway.

Every muscle in my body tenses. My finger rests on the Glock's trigger. The pain in my eyeballs grows sharper.

I almost back down a step or two, but don't want to look weak or be looking up at Clint any more than I already do. As it is, he's already several inches taller. I don't want to give him any more of a psychological advantage.

"Control your dog!" I command.

But Killer's growl grows more fierce.

"You're scaring him," Clint says.

"Yeah, well he's doing a pretty fucking good job of scaring me back," I admit, trying to keep my voice even despite the look of Killer's fangs and the hackles raised on the back of its neck. I'm almost ready to believe that Killer *was* responsible for shredding Katrina Miller, evidence be damned. "Control him, Clint! If he comes after me, I'll put the motherfucker down."

"You hurt my dog, I swear it'll be the last fucking thing you do, McTavish."

I realize belatedly that if Clint has just been buying time so Sheila or someone else could either destroy evidence or bring him a weapon, I've given him that time on a silver platter. But I doubt he's that smart. At least I hope not. And Killer has looked ready to live up to his name.

"Just control your dog," I say, "and quit fucking around. Get your ass out here. You gave me exigent circumstances to come inside, so get out here before I blast my way in."

"Okay, okay," Clint says, then commands, "Easy, Killer."

The dog obeys instantly. It stops growling and closes its mouth. Its ears, formerly at attention, droop. Its raised hackles lie back down. I can see now it's on a leash. Clint puts his hands out through the half-opened door—hands bare except for grasping the leather grip of the leash—and announces that he's coming out. Behind Killer's suddenly calm lead, Clint steps onto the brown welcome mat almost ten feet away.

He's wearing a wifebeater that exposes his massive arms and gut along with black gym shorts and a baseball cap on backwards. From the open doorway, a woman I assume is Sheila holds a phone with both arms outstretched, recording the encounter but with hands shaking so badly the recording will almost certainly be useless. Borderline anorexic with stringy blonde hair, she's wearing only a short white nightgown and panties.

I keep my eyes on Clint and Killer, but speak first to Sheila.

"Sheila, are you okay?"

"What happened to Katrina?" she asks in a shaking voice, partly answering my question by ignoring it.

"That's what I'm trying to find out," I tell her, then turn to Clint. "When I asked you about Katrina, why did you say she was here?"

Clint scratches himself, but shrugs and says nothing.

I nod toward Sheila. "Clint, why did you say that she was Katrina?"

"It's two o'clock in the fucking morning," he says. "I was just trying to get rid of you."

"Where were you tonight?" I ask.

"If you're gonna ask questions like that, I want a lawyer," Clint says, narrowing his eyes. "Come back with a search warrant or I'll let Killer find out if there's anything more than just skin on your scrawny ass."

"He was with me," Sheila says defiantly. "Leave him alone!"

"Shut up, Sheila," Clint says. "We ain't telling him nothin'."

"Sheila," I say sharply, "when I said Katrina was dead, you cried out and said, 'Her too?' Why? Who else?"

"Shut up, Sheila!" Clint says. "I'm warning you!"

"Sheila, I heard you!" I say. "Now, you can answer my question here or I'll take you down to the station in protective custody and you can answer it there. Dumbass here just threatened you. I officially fear for your safety. Now answer my question, what did you mean?"

She puts down the phone and looks at Clint for her answer.

"I didn't mean nothing," she finally says.

The phone in my pocket vibrates. That means Nguyen and Jenkins are on the way.

"Listen, I radioed in my address before I got out of the car," I say. "Two more detectives are a minute or two away. I just got notification on my phone. Now if you want, we can have them bring both of you down to the station for questioning. In separate rooms, of course. In fact, I'd prefer that. That way we can record the whole thing. On the record. So Sheila, please don't say a thing and let me read Clint his rights."

"Liz and Cheryl disappeared," Sheila blurts out. "I'm afraid they're dead. But Clint didn't do nothin' to them."

"*Shut up!*" Clint yells, his eyes bulging out of their sockets.

Killer bares its fangs and strains at its leash.

"You didn't do nothing!" Sheila wails. "You got nothing to hide! Tonight you were with me, and you didn't do nothing to Liz and Cheryl."

Clint gives Sheila a look that tells her what he can't say out loud. Her eyes widen and she begins to shake all over. If she survives the beating Clint has told her will be coming, she might not want to.

"She doesn't know what she's talking about," Clint says, after calming down Killer. "They didn't *disappear*. They just left."

"Did you file a Missing Persons report?" I ask. "I'm guessing not since this is the first I've heard of these two."

Clint shrugs his big shoulders. "Whores leave all the time."

"Right," I say. "And you just let them. It's just like quitting any other job. Like going from Microsoft to Google."

Clint says nothing, but glares at me. Then murderously at Sheila.

In a miracle on par with raising Lazarus from the dead, Jenkins and Nguyen's car finally comes screaming down the street, skids to a noisy stop behind mine, and they come flying out of it.

"McT, you okay?" Nguyen hollers out as she bolts up the walkway, weapon drawn.

Killer goes into a frenzy of barking and straining at its leash, fangs bared.

"Jenkins, call for backup! Two patrol cars!" I yell toward the street. Then to Clint, "Calm your dog now, or I'll calm him for fucking forever."

Clint considers his options for what feels like an eternity, then finally says, "Easy, Killer."

After the first patrol car arrives, we get Killer back inside the house and separate Clint and Sheila. Surrounded by Jenkins and the two patrolmen, Clint stands on the street next to the patrol car, awaiting possible transport to the station downtown. I stand on the porch with Nguyen beside me and Sheila still in the doorway. I convince her that the only thing she can do now to help Clint, and to avoid a possible Accessory charge herself, is to tell me the truth.

"Some of the girls live together in an apartment on Highland Ave," she finally says. "Share the rent, you know? I did too until I moved in here with Clint. Well, two months ago, Liz disappeared and then last month same thing happened with Cheryl. Just up and disappeared. No warning at all. Left Katrina in a real bad way with the rent until some new girl named Julie showed up just two nights ago even though she ain't one of Clint's girls. At least not yet."

"When exactly did Liz and Cheryl disappear?"

"A month apart is all I know."

"Taken by a john?"

"Don't know. They went to work one night and never came home."

I get the exact address and apartment on Highland from Sheila, as well as the full names for Liz Delgado, Cheryl McNulty, and Julie Winston. And when Sheila has told all she has to tell, I say that we've got to bring Clint in for more questioning. Three girls in three months can't be a coincidence. And based on how he was looking at her, she might want to find another place to stay for a while and lay low.

---

THE APARTMENT on Highland is on the top floor of a decrepit triple-decker that poses a danger to anyone who steps inside. Rats squeal in the walls of the curving wooden staircase. Every third or fourth step threatens to give way due to advancing decay. It reeks of urine. Outside, gutters dangle unattached. The second- and third-floor side porches sag so precariously only a daredevil or a meth head would venture onto them or trust their rotting railings.

I don't notice it at first because of all the other rank odors, but as I pound on the door, I belatedly sense the pronounced smell of dog in the hallway. Initially, I wonder if it's all in my head, but I realize it isn't.

*Dog.*

I suppose it shouldn't be that surprising. Plenty of people own dogs. Even meth head prostitutes. But this smell is so strong, and so coincidental with what happened to Katrina Miller that it can't be mere coincidence, can it?

Although it isn't *exactly* a dog smell either. Close, but different. And much stronger.

Unless it really is all in my head.

I pound on the door even more frantically while also drawing my Glock.

But if Julie Winston is inside that apartment—if she's *alive* and inside the apartment—there's no way of telling. I pound and pound, but no amount of banging on the door gets her to answer. All I succeed in doing is waking up and pissing off the residents of the first two floors, who yell angrily at me, then refuse to answer my questions. None of them knows anything. None of them is the super with a master key.

Nguyen and Jenkins are revising the search warrant application to use this address instead of the years-old one from the DMV, and there's no chance it'll get rejected. So, I'm not going to break the door down and taint the scene. I'll come back later.

<hr>

I KNOCK AGAIN on the door at nine that morning, my suit now quite rumpled. I'm armed with a warrant and ready to call in specialists with a battering ram, if necessary.

Instead, a healthy, athletic-looking young woman answers the door.

She's everything that Katrina Miller was not. No meth mouth but instead a beautiful set of teeth. A clear complexion. Long, flowing blonde hair so light it borders on being white. Vibrant, piercing eyes.

Alive in a way that Katrina's eyes had been dead for as long as I'd known her. Piercing as if accusing me of not preventing Katrina's death.

"Come in, Detective McTavish," she says with a husky voice that reminds me of Emma Stone.

I blink. "How did you know who I am?"

"You've got a search warrant in your hand and you're well known as the senior detective on the force."

I step inside, surprised at my notoriety among civilians. Once again, I sense the distinct smell of dog. Or almost-dog.

Unless it's all in my head. Or it hasn't left my nostrils since the crime scene and perhaps never will.

The apartment opens on a tiny dining room with a square bare metal table surrounded by four chairs. Water stains dot the aging wallpaper. A wall clock ticks loudly. A bedroom and bathroom are to my left. Behind me, adjacent to the front door, a kitchen. Up ahead, a hallway to what I assume are other bedrooms and a possible living room.

"Are you Julie Winston?"

"Yes," she says. We take seats at opposite ends of the table. "I've been expecting you for some time now."

"How long?"

"Since a little after Katrina Miller's death."

My head snaps back as if slapped. A half dozen questions jump instantly to the tip of my tongue.

I start slow. "You were here at a little after two a.m.?"

"Yes, but I was indisposed, you might say," she says.

"You couldn't possibly have slept through my banging on your door. I woke up the entire house, all three floors except for this one."

She smiles grimly. "You might say I'm a heavy sleeper."

I take that to mean pills or heroin, although she looks far too healthy for the latter. I move on.

"You said you'd been waiting for me since Katrina Miller's death. Exactly what time do you think that was?"

"She was attacked at midnight and died within seconds."

I'm stunned. I try to maintain a poker face even while mentally, at least, my jaw drops. The tip line got the call exactly one minute after midnight, the first patrol car arrived three minutes later, followed by Nguyen and Jenkins, an additional patrol car, and then myself. The ME's initial time of death estimate was sometime between 11:30 and midnight.

"How do you know when she was attacked and died?"

"Because I was there."

Another shocker. There's no maintaining a poker face now. I stare at this woman with her matter-of-fact admission. "You were there?"

She averts her eyes. "I called it in right after she died. It's my voice on your tip line. You can check it."

I recall Jenkins's words now about the call. "A female voice with a husky, masculine edge." And when I'd heard this woman's first words inside this apartment, I thought of Emma Stone. Maybe not masculine, but definitely husky.

"You didn't call until *after* she was dead?" I ask.

"I was supposed to stop it," Julie says, looking downcast. "I failed. He overpowered me."

"*Who* overpowered you?"

She purses her lips and swallows hard. "Lucas."

"Lucas who? What's his full name?"

She shakes her head. "Just Lucas."

"I need his full name! Name and address!"

Julie takes a very long time answering. I hear the wall clock going *tick, tick, tick.*

Then *tick, tick, tick.*

And *tick, tick, tick.*

Finally, she says, "You're not going to believe me. You'll think I'm crazy."

"Try me," I say.

"Lucas is from the *Unter Stadt*. The Under City, just like me."

I swear under my breath. I've been wasting my fucking time. Getting my hopes up. But she's just another whack job. No different than all the other lunatics who call tip lines and swear they shot JFK, or killed Jimmy Hoffa, or kidnapped the Lindbergh baby.

This Julie Winston really had me going. Clear-eyed and sober. Everything Katrina was not.

*Unter Stadt*, my ass.

I stare at her and shake my head. "I don't have time for your bullshit. Now let me search this place."

"Search it all you want," she says. "Doubt me all you

want. But tell me this. How did I know what time Katrina died if I wasn't there? My voice is on your tip line. And I'll tell you how Lucas killed her."

"How?" I ask, the bitter taste of disappointment in my mouth.

"He tore her apart with his claws, then he ate her neck and shoulders."

I can only stare, wide-eyed.

"Lucas is a werewolf," she says, fixing me with her eyes. "Just like me."

When I sit there frozen and say nothing, she adds, "The rest of our kind are no danger to your people. Only Lucas has gone rogue and is beyond our control. Only Lucas has killed humans. Three times. On the last three full moons.

"The first two times, he dragged his victims down into the *Unter Stadt* and savaged them there. So, you failed to notice. But his disease grows with every day. He can control it no longer. So this last time, you saw the full force of his savagery. And you will see if again if you cannot stop him."

I shake my head in disbelief.

"Let me ask you this," Julie says, her voice even more husky now, and the smell of almost-dog—*of wolf!*—filling the room. "Where did those bloody paw prints lead? They went all the way to the other side of the tracks. To the rock wall and the dragon and 'JoJo + Paul.' To the portal to the *Unter Stadt.*"

Twenty-nine days later, I lie in wait for Lucas. Overhead, a full moon dominates the darkened sky. Silver bullets fill my long-range rifle. I crouch hidden inside an abandoned old brick warehouse several hundred feet from the rock wall that opens to the *Unter Stadt*. All the warehouse's windows are boarded up except for one. When I look through the scope of my rifle past the empty parking lot, I clearly see the colorful dragon, its hues of yellow and blue and red altered by the orange glow of the streetlights. "JoJo + Paul" is as easy for me to read as the top line in an eye chart.

I do not, of course, have the official sanction of the Bleektown Police Force or the mayor or any elected official for what I am about to do. I don't have an unofficial blessing or even the knowledge of a single individual.

I'm on my own. The way I work best.

I withheld my belief in what was surely the tallest of tall tales until I could deny it no longer. I listened to the voice on the tip line. I aligned the dates of Liz Delgado and Cheryl McNulty's disappearances with the full moon. I compared the tattered ribbons of Katrina's skin with the spacing of the claws in the bloody paw prints. The hair samples and bloody paw prints collected matched no earthly dog, coyote, or even wolf, and there has been only a single wolf sighting in this state in the last century, and certainly none close to an urban center like Bleektown.

DNA samples from the crime scene have not yet been analyzed—three dead whores don't qualify for a rush— but I'm guessing when they are analyzed, we'll hear of corrupted samples since they don't match either human or wolf, only a mix.

My doubts still held sway, though, despite my decades-long instinctive discomfort around the train station's rock wall until Julie broke the most sacred of *Unter Stadt* rules. She allowed me to watch her, unconcealed, stand up against the colorful dragon on the rock wall, press herself against "JoJo + Paul," and melt into the stone.

Back to the *Unter Stadt.*

The mayor and police chief have complained about my failure to resolve the case with phrases like "not even a whore deserves to die like that," and coded suggestions that I pin Katrina's savage killing on "the usual suspects." Mostly, though, they've conspired to keep the grisly details under wraps so as to "not overly alarm the good people of this city."

Which means if I succeed this evening undetected, life in Bleektown will return to its usual cesspool self. If I'm found out, I'll spend the rest of my life in a psychiatric hospital, and officials will comment privately that they'd always wondered about me.

If I fail, Lucas will find his next Katrinas with every full moon.

I have been assured that no other werewolves—none of the "safe" werewolves—will venture through the portal this evening despite the full moon. Only Lucas. His distinctive long white stripe on the left side of an otherwise gray coat will identify him clearly.

I wait patiently, the smell of the disrupted rat droppings filling the heavy air. The last train rumbled out of the station almost half an hour ago at 11:10, but still no Lucas.

Finally, though, the dragon on the rock wall grows cloudy and indistinct. It remains that way through my rifle scope for several long seconds. I draw in a breath, then exhale. My finger grows warm on the trigger.

Lucas emerges.

At first, it is in humanoid fashion, its back to the dragon on the rock wall, and I'm tempted to think of it as a man. Not *it*, but *he*.

Then I remember what it did to Katrina Miller and Liz Delgado and Cheryl McNulty. Lucas will never be a *him*. Lucas is an *it*.

It turns sideways looking for the moon. Euphoria fills its face as it finds it.

Thick gray fur sprouts all over its body, covering it save for the distinctive long white stripe on its left that assures me this is indeed Lucas.

My finger tightens on the trigger.

Lucas reaches its arms out to the moon and extends its claws. It opens its mouth to cry out, its white fangs glistening.

I pull the trigger.

The first shot hits Lucas square in the chest and slams its body against the rock wall.

*That's for Katrina Miller.*

I pull the trigger again. This time it's a head shot that blows off Lucas's emerging snout.

*For Liz Delgado.*

And as Lucas slides slowly down the wall, my third shot takes off the rest of its head.

*For Cheryl McNulty.*

By the time I place my rifle on the warehouse floor, pull off my rubber gloves, and race out of the warehouse and to the body, Lucas has reverted fully to humanoid form.

Still very dead, but a dead human. Much easier to explain than a dead werewolf.

For the first time, I consider a death on my watch to be addition by subtraction.

Part of a much-needed cleansing process.

Thank you for your interest in my books.

DHH

# NEWSLETTER

Be the first to know!

If you love my writing, my newsletter is a great way to keep up with new releases, special promotions, and other content that's only available to my newsletter subscribers.

What are you waiting for?

Sign up at www.hendricksonwriter.com/newsletter-free-story/ today!

# ALSO BY DAVID H. HENDRICKSON

**Novels: Romance**

*Body Check*

*No Defense*

*Romantic Concerto for Strings and Brass*

**Novels: Young Adult/Sports/Historical**

*Cracking the Ice*

*Offside*

*Offensive Foul*

*Bottom of the Ninth*

*The Rabbit Labelle Trilogy (Omnibus)*

**Novels: Humor/Crime**

*Bubba Goes for Broke*

**Novels: Mystery/Suspense**

*Pain Train (forthcoming)*

**Collections**

*Shimmers and Laughs: Eight Wildly Hilarious Tales*

*Death in the Serengeti and Other Stories: Ten Tales of Crime*

*The Boy in the Boxers and Other Stories of Sweet Romance*

*Hell of a Band: Twelve Fantasy Stories*

*Fighting the Dying Light: Stories of Aging*

*Cape Cod Chips, Wiener Dogs, and Swiping Left: Stories of Sweet Romance*

*The Soulmate Junkie and Other Stories of Fantasy & Science Fiction*

*Crime From Another Time: Stories of Mystery and Suspense* (forthcoming)

*Crime Fantastique: Stories of Mystery and Suspense* (forthcoming)

*Crime, Up Close and Personal: Stories of Mystery and Suspense* (forthcoming)


**Nonfiction**

*How to Get Your Book Into Schools and Double Your Income With Volume Sales*

*Travis Roy: Quadriplegia and a Life of Purpose*

*Hendu's Story: From Dream to Reality*

# ACKNOWLEDGMENTS

To Dean Wesley Smith, Leah Cutter, Annie Reed, Jamie Ferguson, and Kerrie L. Hughes, the editors who believed in these stories.

To Annie Reed, the editor and cover designer of this collection, whose expertise, advice, and friendship I can always rely on.

To my readers, whose enthusiasm helps keep me going.

To my family and friends, who support me during the valleys and celebrate with me on the mountaintops.

And above all, to Brenda, The Best Wife Ever™, for always being there and filling life's journey with such joy.

# ABOUT THE AUTHOR

David H. Hendrickson's first novel, *Cracking the Ice*, was praised by *Booklist* as "a gripping account of a courageous young man rising above evil." He has since published seven additional novels, including *Offside*, which has been adopted for high school student required reading.

His short fiction has appeared in *Best American Mystery Stories 2018*, *Ellery Queen's Mystery Magazine*, *Thrill Ride - the Magazine*, *Heart's Kiss*, almost every issue of *Pulphouse Fiction Magazine* and *Mystery, Crime, and Mayhem*, as well as numerous anthologies, including over a half dozen issues of *Fiction River*. He is a multi-finalist for the Derringer Award, and his story "Death in the Serengeti" was honored with the 2018 Derringer Award for Best Long Story.

He has published nine short story collections with another forthcoming. Currently available: *Shimmers and Laughs: Eight Wildly Hilarious Tales*; *Death in the Serengeti and Other Stories: Ten Tales of Crime*; *The Boy in the Boxers and Other Stories of Sweet Romance*; *Hell of a Band: Twelve Fantasy Stories*; *Fighting the Dying Light: Stories of Aging*; *Cape Cod Chips, Wiener Dogs, and Swiping Left: Stories of Sweet Romance*; *The Soulmate Junkie and Other Stories of Fantasy & Science Fiction*; *Crime from Another Time: Stories* of *Mystery and Suspense*, and *Crime Fantastique: Stories of Mystery and Suspense*.

Hendrickson has published over fifteen hundred works of nonfiction, most notably his first book for writers, *How to Get Your Book into Schools and Double Your Income with Volume Sales*, and also *Travis Roy: Quadriplegia and a Life of Purpose* and *Hendu's Story: From Dream to Reality*. He has been honored with the Joe Concannon Hockey East Media Award and the Murray Kramer Scarlet Quill Award.

Visit him online at www.hendricksonwriter.com.

www.ingramcontent.com/pod-product-compliance
Lightning Source LLC
Chambersburg PA
CBHW031751200726
48289CB00013B/788